Nemesis for the Judge

Judge Wes Talbot was the youngest circuit judge in the history of the territory, a fact of which he was mightily proud, considering that he had started out as an enforcer of the law, rather than a dispenser of justice.

When Wes had tried Dan Meldrum, the defendant in the infamous Concord Massacre case, the evidence had been damning. Finding him guilty of rape and murder Wes had sentenced him to be hanged. Yet Cash Meldrum, the bounty hunter known as the Deacon, is convinced of his brother's innocence and sets out to make the judge pay. But then fate plays a hand and a gang of outlaws kidnaps Talbot's fiancée and her best friend. Now Wes himself is forced on the run and as events close in it surely looks like *Nemesis for the Judge*.

Nemesis for the Judge

CLAY MORE

A Black Horse Western

ROBERT HALE · LONDON

© Clay More 2004
First published in Great Britain 2004

ISBN 0 7090 7605 3

Robert Hale Limited
Clerkenwell House
Clerkenwell Green
London EC1R 0HT

Typeset by
Derek Doyle & Associates, Liverpool.
Printed and bound in Great Britain by
Antony Rowe Limited, Wiltshire

For Miss Mollie – always a good judge

PROLOGUE

Governor Earl Grady puffed nervously on his pipe as he watched the man in black sitting on the other side of his desk. For a full five minutes the man had sat reading his dead brother's journal, written with a stub of pencil over the course of a week in the condemned cell, before his execution by hanging.

The governor had overseen the penitentiary for twenty years, had known many hundred violent, cruel and just plain bad men, yet Cash Meldrum, renowned throughout the Southwest as 'the Deacon', made him feel especially nervous. A bounty hunter with at least fifteen slayings to his tally, his apparent lack of emotion was disquietingly incongruous.

Then suddenly, steely-blue eyes were turned on the governor.

'You read this?'

Earl Grady gulped smoke, grimaced despite

himself and laid his pipe down. 'I have. Regulations demand that I read all communications written by a condemned man.'

The steely eyes stared unblinkingly at him, causing a cold shiver to run down his spine, as if he was being sized up by a poisonous reptile.

'Danny didn't do any of these things,' said the Deacon. 'My little brother never told a lie in his life. He didn't kill anybody and he didn't rape no woman.'

The governor cleared his throat, reached over and pulled the official file back across the desk. 'Mr Meldrum, you've read the report of the case proceedings. The court found your brother guilty of the killing of the driver of the overland stage from Hacksville and of two male passengers – a whiskey drummer and a farmer – and of the rape, along with two other men, of the local banker's wife on her way home from visiting a sick relative.'

The Deacon shook his head. 'Danny was just twenty years old, Governor. He wrote to tell me that he was proud as hell of landing that job of messenger-guard on the stage run. He was brought up to be respectful of women. There's just no way he could have done it.'

'The evidence and testimony of the raped woman indicates that he was part of a planned robbery by a local gang that call themselves the Rough Riders. After they raped the woman –

brutally, I might say – they shared a bottle of whiskey, then fell out.'

The Deacon clicked his tongue. 'And Danny was found dead drunk at the scene with a bump on his head. That don't seem to tie up, Governor.'

Earl Grady sat up stiffly. 'The woman testified against him, Mr Meldrum. There was no doubt. You read Judge Talbot's summing up.'

The Deacon nodded. 'I read it, and it stinks. He sent an innocent man to the gallows!'

The governor had begun flicking through the file to find the appropriate page with the judge's findings and sentence, but Cash Meldrum was already on his feet. 'I just want to see my brother's body now.'

The smell of death pervaded the whole of the dank corridor that led to the mortuary, where a single rough coffin lay atop a trestle table. The governor gestured to the weather-beaten, bucolic-looking guard who had accompanied them from the office. 'Open the coffin,' he snapped, now anxious for the bounty hunter to see his brother's body and take it away.

The guard prised open the lid and held it back for the Deacon to see the body of the young man who lay within. Dressed in a simple muslin shroud, head at a slightly unnatural angle, the face was clearly a younger version of Cash Meldrum's.

For the first time the Deacon showed slight emotion. A jaw muscle twitched and his clenched knuckles went white.

'Did he die right?'

The guard nodded his head with respect and with a degree of professional satisfaction. 'He didn't kick up no fuss and the hanging was perfect and painless. Broke his neck straight away.'

The Deacon drew out a small leather bag and fished out three silver dollars. He tossed one to the guard. 'I'd appreciate it if'n you'd give that to the hangman.' Then he turned back to the body of his brother and smoothed a strand of hair off his forehead.

'They did you injustice, Danny,' he said, as he laid a silver dollar on each closed eye. 'I'll bring you justice, boy.' He bowed his head then whispered, '" *Vengeance is mine; I will repay, saith the Lord*".'

Then with a final nod he turned for the door, much to the governor's surprise.

'Mr Meldrum, aren't you going to take your brother's body?'

The Deacon shook his head. 'I've paid my respects, Governor. Bury him in the pen's cemetery.' He patted his thighs where his holsters normally lay. 'All I want now is to get my ironware back, and then I'll be going.'

Five minutes later, Cash Meldrum mounted his horse, then nodded down at the governor, who was all too clearly relieved to see him leave.

'What was the name of that judge again?'

'Judge Wesley Talbot,' Governor Earl Grady replied.

The Deacon rode out before the governor had the opportunity to ask why he wanted to know. Striking a light to his pipe, he reflected that maybe it was better not to know the answer to that particular question.

ONE

The Concord lurched along the undulating semi-desert trail, through tracts of sand and towering red rock formations, then across boulder-strewn plains where only mesquite and saguaro cactus thrived, until it reached the edge of the Pintos Mountains where it straightened up and ran parallel with the chain of foothills.

Passing through copses of scrub-oak and paloverde, where gunmen could easily lie waiting, Ben Tupper, the weather-beaten driver, flicked his bullwhip to induce the span of three horses to pick up speed, then dug the messenger in the ribs, urging him to have his shotgun ready, just in case. The sun beat down from a cloudless, cobalt sky, parching everything, from desert spadefoot to husky old coach driver, and Ben promised himself that he was going to down at least two beers, provided they got to Hacksville unmolested.

Sitting inside, a fine patina of dust having accumulated on them through the glassless windows, the passengers reflexly banked and swayed with every movement of the stagecoach. After a day of enforced companionship they had long since used up all of their polite conversation and lapsed into semi-stuporous apathy. Or at least that is how it may have seemed.

Judge Wes Talbot, a tall black-haired thirty-year-old fellow, the youngest circuit judge in the history of the territory, sat with his Stetson pulled low over his face, as if asleep. In reality, however, he was ready to reach for the Remington-Elliot 'pepper-box' in his shoulder holster at the first sign of trouble. It was not that the two handsome women or the crabby elderly preacher posed any threat, it was a natural vigilance, superstition maybe, on account of the fact that they were travelling in the very stage that had recently been robbed and its driver and passengers killed and one of them raped.

Wes Talbot knew all this only too well, for it was only a month previously that he had tried the case in Hacksville – and sentenced the messenger of the Concord to be hanged.

A high-pitched whistle from the roof of the Concord followed by a string of invective from Ben Tupper preceded a slowing down as the trail dropped into a gully and the stage began to descend. Almost immediately, a wheel caught a deep rut and the stage lurched violently, ejecting the younger of the two women from her seat and propelling her on to Wes's lap.

The two women giggled coquettishly as Wes sat up with a start, catching her in his arms to prevent her ricocheting on to the floor between the seats.

'Hold on, folks!' the driver cried belatedly.

'We just hit a pothole,' the messenger explained unnecessarily.

Rudely awakened from his slumber, the elderly preacher eyed Wes and the young woman sitting on his lap with disapproval.

'I beg your pardon, sir,' the girl said, raising a hand to the feather toque on her head. 'I wouldn't want you to think that I sit on strangers' knees uninvited, like this.' She beamed at him with the merest suggestion of a wink before retaking her seat opposite him.

'Don't think about it, ma'am,' replied Wes, tilting his hat.

The older woman, a pretty brunette of about Wes's age shook her head. 'Don't tell her that, mister. She's been thinking about sitting on your knee ever since we boarded this stage. She's just getting in some practice for her new job.'

'You've got new jobs in Hacksville?' Wes asked quickly, embarrassment causing his cheeks to burn.

'We surely do, sir,' the raven-haired younger woman replied. 'We're singers and we're going to work in the Lucky Belle Saloon. Maybe you'll come and visit us there?' She pointed to the bulge under Wes's coat where his pepperbox lay in its holster. 'I see you're a man of action.' She smiled again, enunciating her words deliberately. 'All prepared and everything.'

Blushing despite himself, Wes smiled at her. 'Maybe I will, ma'am. Maybe I will.'

The elderly preacher snorted disdainfully, turned and closed his eyes.

'Get ready, folks,' came Ben Tupper's voice almost immediately. 'We'll be in Hacksville in five minutes.'

Sheriff Henry Logan was leaning on a post as the passengers disembarked and collected their luggage, which the messenger unceremoniously tossed down into the dirt of the town main street.

'Judge Talbot,' said the sheriff, straightening up as Wes turned with his bag. 'I'm sure glad to see you.'

The two female passengers opened their eyes in surprise. 'Why, Betsy,' said the brunette, 'I had no idea we were riding with a judge. And you jumping on him like a real hussy!'

Betsy giggled. 'Best to start on the right side of the law, Laura dear. That's all I was doing.'

And with a simultaneous 'Bye Judge,' they ambled away in the direction of the Lucky Belle Saloon, their bustles swaying provocatively, which did not go unnoticed by the crowd of male loafers

15

who had gathered to see who had come to town.

Wes grinned as he shook the sheriff's hand. 'Good to see you again, Henry.' Then he frowned. 'But you look worried. Have you got another difficult case for me?'

Logan pointed across the street. 'You obviously haven't heard about the killings,' he said softly. 'Maybe we'd best have a chat before you head off to the hotel.'

Every time Wes stepped inside a sheriff's office and breathed in the mixed aroma of leather, ironware and the stale body odour from recent occupants of the cells, he felt himself transported back a few years. For Wes had spent much of his youth as a lawman in various cow towns across the territory. It had only been after a discussion with the late governor that he had headed East to study jurisprudence in order to move up a notch. Instead of merely enforcing the law, he now dispensed justice. He enjoyed the nomadic life of a circuit judge, travelling from town to town, hearing cases, using his brain instead of his gun to bring justice to the ungodly fleshpots of the Southwest.

He sat in the proffered seat beside the gun rack and surveyed the posters of wanted felons. The profusion of them emphasized the problem that faced lawmen in this part of the world. Yet as he watched Henry Logan pour coffee from the ever-ready pot he also realized how fortunate the townspeople of Hacksville were. Although the town was such a short distance from the Pintos foothills, a veritable maze of canyons, gulches and gullies inhabited by numerous gangs and solitary outlaws, such was the reputation of the tough sheriff that the town was kept relatively free of trouble.

In the tied-down holster at his hip rested Logan's famous Le Mat revolver. Not made for fast drawing, it was virtually a one-man artillery piece. With nine shots in its cylinder for shooting from its regular barrel, it also had beneath an 18-gauge shotgun barrel for its tenth shot. A man had to be brave, stupid or probably both to go up against Henry Logan.

Wes accepted the cup of strong black Arbuckle's and sipped appreciatively, as it helped to take the cake of swallowed dust from the back of his mouth. He watched Logan dump himself in the swivel chair behind his desk and take a hefty sip. 'It's bad, Wes,' he said at last. 'Five killings and I reckon they're all related to the Concord Massacre.'

Wes raised his eyebrows. The recent case he had tried had become infamous across the territory as the Concord Massacre, thanks mainly to the reporting style of the *Hacksville Chronicle*, the local newspaper that was distributed to all the towns along the length of the Pintos. Wes had some reservations about the journalistic style, but welcomed the coming of the newspaper as a sign that civilization was reaching this part of the world.

Logan recounted how five men had been murdered in the surrounding area over the past two weeks. All five of them had been members of the jury that heard the Concord Massacre case. They had all been shot in their homes or in isolated spots out of town.

'Anybody killed here in Hacksville?'

Logan shook his head. 'They've all been home-steaders or ranchers. The jury was made up half and half. Half townsfolk, half outliers.' He puffed his cheeks. 'It's got everyone round here pretty well spooked. The sixth outlier just upped and offed last week, afore death came knocking at his door. As for the townsfolk, there's some pressure on me to approach the military.'

Wes produced a cigar case from his jacket and proffered it. When they both had smoke going, he asked, 'Any clues to who's behind it?'

The door opened and a bespectacled, portly, middle-aged man wearing a brown apron covered in ink, with rolled up sleeves burst in unan-nounced. He had mutton-chop whiskers and smoked a charred pipe. 'Clues? 'Course he's got clues. Haven't you told him, Logan?'

Then, before the sheriff could get a word in, he crossed the office and held out a meaty hand. 'Good to see you, Wes, but how come you haven't read any of this in the *Chronicle*.' He gave a mock frown. 'Goddamit, I work my fingers to the bone writing, printing and producing the best damned paper in the area – no, the only paper in the area – and then I send it to every town within fifty miles of here, and you have the gall to admit that you haven't read it!'

Wes grinned at Phineas Bradley, known to all as Phin, the local printer, editor and proprietor of the *Hacksville Chronicle*. 'I see you've been doing your usual snooping for news by listening at doors. But if you'd let a man get a word in, I'd explain. The thing is that your paper doesn't reach everywhere, you old reprobate. I go to places where the only news people are interested in is whether they're still alive at the end of the day. Now what clues are you talking about?'

Phin Bradley looked at Sheriff Logan, who scrutinized the end of his cigar. 'It's kinda sick, Wes,' the sheriff said. 'The killer has left silver dollars on the eyes of the victims. You know of anyone who does that?'

Wes shook his head.

'It's the trade mark of Cash Meldrum,' Phin interrupted, keen to get the story told. 'Whether it's a superstition he has or what, no one knows. He's got religion of a sort, folk say. They call him the Deacon.'

'He's Daniel Meldrum's brother, Wes,' Logan explained. 'You sentenced him to be hanged.'

Wes whistled softly. 'Of course! And this Deacon, is he an outlaw?'

Logan shook his head. 'Bounty hunter. His

19

other trade mark – that Phin didn't mention – is that he never takes a man in alive if he can help it. And it sure looks as if he's set on getting revenge for his little brother – by killing everyone who had a hand in getting him hanged.'

That evening, after a bath, shave and rest at the Hacksville Grand Hotel, Wes joined Logan and Phin for dinner at the newspaperman's home. A widower, Phin was looked after, spoilt most folk averred, by his daughter Pam Bradley. An auburn beauty with the bluest eyes imaginable, she had clearly inherited her mother's good looks.

'Judge Talbot came into town with a couple of lady admirers,' Logan jested, as Pam served steaks to her seated guests.

'Did he now?' she said, glancing at Wes, two slight touches of colour forming on her cheeks as he looked up and smiled at her.

Logan grinned to himself, seeing confirmation of feelings between them that he had suspected before. 'Yes ma'am, a couple of real beauties just starting at the Lucky Belle Saloon.'

'Singers,' Wes explained. Then, turning to Phin Bradley he asked, 'Is that worth a piece in the *Hacksville Chronicle?*'

The newspaperman chuckled as he made a start on his steak. 'Everything that happens in Hacksville, from a dog fouling the boardwalk to news of a court hearing is newsworthy, Wes. People want to know what's happening in the area. Nothing is too trivial. Two new singers arriving in town will surely demand me checking out the Lucky Belle someday soon.'

Pam sipped her drink. 'These killings have everyone talking at the moment. I've interviewed about twenty people in the last two weeks and everyone's scared witless.'

Wes nodded. Pam Bradley not only looked after Phineas Bradley's home, but she helped him report news, as well as set print and operate the patent rotary printer that produced the *Hacksville Chronicle.*

'How is Mrs Bolton, the banker's wife?' Wes asked.

Pam shook her head. 'She was petrified before the first killing, which is understandable, considering she'd been raped by those monsters. Now she hardly dares go out, unless it's with her husband, Dexter, or me. She's mostly doped up to the eyeballs with sedatives from Doc Munro.'

Logan finished chewing a mouthful of steak and laid his fork down for a moment. 'I guess she's feeling it bad, just like the other members of the jury who live in town. She'll be thinking the killer is going to come for her, especially since it was her testimony that convicted Daniel Meldrum.' Then, sensing an embarrassed silence as he spoke, Logan gave a short laugh in an attempt to lighten the mood at the dinner-table. He patted the Le Mat strapped to his side. 'But that's why I'm here. I'm sworn to protect the people of this town, and that's just what I aim to do.'

Phin Bradley nodded. 'And we need to watch your back too, Henry. I expect the Deacon won't be too keen on the sheriff who arrested his brother and transferred him to the pen to be hung.'

Pam Bradley looked at Wes with concern written across her face. 'And that means that the judge who sentenced his brother is bound to be top of his hate list.'

The rest of the evening passed convivially. After coffee, whiskey and cigars, Wes and the sheriff took their leave. After agreeing on a time to meet next morning to look at the cases he needed to consider in the town's makeshift courtroom, they went their separate ways. Wes went back to his hotel, while Logan set off on his nightly round of the town.

Wes fell asleep almost as soon as his head hit the pillow. But it was a troubled sleep that he fell into. He dreamed that he was outside, in front of a large crowd, finding a man guilty of murder and rape, then passing sentence. 'Hang him!' he cried in his sleep. Yet there was doubt in his mind. No sooner had he sentenced the young man, than he was aware that he doubted his own judgment. Only now it was too late, for the crowd had shoved the man up into his saddle and slipped a noose round his neck. Then guns were being fired, scaring the horse, which galloped away, leaving the man dangling, kicking convulsively.

The gunfire grew louder, the crowd shouted louder and louder, and he grew ever more anxious about his judgment.

Galloping hooves woke him and he bolted upright in his bed, as the hooves receded into the background. But not so the gunfire and the cries of the crowd.

Flickering light shone through the window and in a trice he was out of bed and peering down. A little further along the street the sheriff's office was on fire; its clapboard walls turning it into a raging inferno that none of the gathering crowd could approach. Apart from which, shots kept ringing out from the blaze as ammunition inside the office went off spontaneously in the heat of the fire.

It was not until daybreak when the flames had died completely and the final cartridge had exploded that anyone could enter the razed building. Wes Talbot and Phin Bradley were among the first to see the grisly spectacle.

The stench of burned flesh had a gut-twisting effect on everyone, matched only by the sight of the charred body. It was lying on its back, arms outstretched with a gaping hole in the chest just below the half-melted sheriff's badge. Mercifully, if such a word could be used in reference to cold-blooded murder, it looked as if death had claimed him before the fire was started. The flesh had burned to charcoal, making the features unrecognizable. Yet it was the presence of the two silver dollars that had been laid over the eyes that sent chills up everyone's spine.

'Poor Henry,' said Wes, picking up the still hot Le Mat that lay half out of the charred leather holster. 'Looks like he tried to defend himself, but just didn't make it.'

Phin made the sign of a cross in the air. 'God rest his soul,' he said. Then under his breath: 'And God help us all.'

TWO

Cash Meldrum was dog-tired from riding all night. He had bitterness in his heart and he wanted to kill, to extract life from whoever had been responsible for taking the life of his kid brother. He didn't care how many there were, he'd make them all pay – especially one!

Shortly after daybreak he found a place to rest: a clearing by a river, sheltered from prying eyes by spruce and tangles of scrub-oak, with enough grass on the bank to keep his bay happy while he breakfasted and then slept.

With a fire built and a pot of coffee bubbling away to make the thick concentrated brew that he favoured, he had stripped to the waist, shed his ironware and boots, then crawled to the edge of the bank where he lay flat, a hand trailing in the water. Although he had salted pork in his saddlebag, the sight of shoals of silver-scaled fish sheltering in the shadows of the bank had made his taste buds tingle.

It was patient work, which suited him at that moment, for he was conscious of the inner rage that needed to be quenched. And as he tickled the belly of a fair-sized trout, he was transported back to the days of his youth, to a similar sun-baked day by a creek, when he had taught Danny to fish this way.

'Tickle them slow, make them feel special, at ease,' he whispered, as if his brother was lying beside him now. His hand moved slowly along the length of the fish, his fingers forming into a cup. 'Then flick her out!' he said to his imagined brother, whom he saw in his mind's eye grinning at him, soaking up his teaching. And as he performed the manoeuvre, flicking a good two-pounder in an arc out of the water to land wriggling and gasping on the bank, the spell was broken. His brother's face disappeared, replaced by the stark image of him lying in his coffin. He forced the image away as he picked up the wriggling fish and dispatched its life with a sharp crack on a stone. A few deft movements with his short Bowie-knife and the fish was gutted and deposited in his waiting pan.

Wiping the blade clean he sheathed the knife and looked skywards. 'Thank you, Lord, for providing this bounty.' And being a particular sort of cove, he turned and waded into the water until he was in up to his waist in the cool refreshing water, then he began sluicing himself clean of the accumulated grime and trail dirt.

There came the sound of a gun hammer being ratcheted back, and then a sarcastic voice barked, 'And the Lord be thanked for providing us with this *bounty hunter*! Now, Preacher, turn round real slow!'

The whole town had been buzzing with the news of the burning down of the jailhouse and the brutal slaying of Sheriff Henry Logan. Phin and Pam Bradley were already hard at work composing the main story for the next edition of the *Hacksville Chronicle*. To Pam it almost seemed to be a cold-blooded thing to do, especially since Henry Logan had supped at table with them the night before, but her father had consoled her and counselled her upon the importance of doing a first-class professional job both to honour their late friend and sheriff, and to provide folks with information that might help to bring his murderer to justice.

Wes Talbot stopped by the office on his way to the courthouse, and was inevitably button-holed by Phin for an on-the-spot interview from 'the Judge who had shared so many cases with Sheriff Logan'. Shortly after Wes left, Dexter Bolton came rushing into the newspaper office to see Pam. He was a tall stick of a man dressed in a sober grey suit. Of an anxious disposition, he had serious frown lines on his brow and the wispy moustache he grew long to cover partially his mouth and crooked teeth only served to emphasize his weak chin.

'Pam, I hate to ask you, but could you call round and see Evelyn?' he asked, screwing his hat in his hands.

'Is she ill, Dexter?' Phin asked concernedly, looking up from his compositor and cleaning his hands on a rag.

'She's worse'n ever,' the banker replied. 'As soon as she heard about Sheriff Logan, God rest his soul, she's gone plumb hysterical. She's sure that murdering swine is going to come looking for her. She locked herself in the bathroom this morning and wouldn't come out until I fetched Doc Munro. He's with her now, giving her a sedative of some sort.' He turned to Pam. 'She's in a real state, Pam. She begged me to come and ask you to visit.' His knuckles grew white, threatening to squeeze his hat completely out of shape. 'I'd consider it a real favour if you'd drop by.'

Phin nodded to his daughter, as if to reassure her that he could cope with the newspaper.

'Of course I'll come, Dexter,' Pam said. 'Evelyn's my best friend.'

Dexter Bolton bobbed his head. 'Thanks, Pam.' He donned his dishevelled hat and edged awkwardly towards the door. 'I've gotta open the bank now, but I'll be back home in an hour.'

When Pam let herself into the banker's home

ten minutes later, Doc Munro was putting a glass syringe back into his black medical bag. He looked up as Pam closed the door behind her and puffed up his cheeks to signal his relief at her arrival.

'Thanks for coming, Pam,' he said softly. 'I reckon your presence is going to be more useful than the injection I've just given her.' He nodded towards the bedroom where Pam could see Evelyn Bolton's feet lying on top of the big double bed.

At the sound of Pam's name, the feet were swung off the bed and a moment later Evelyn Bolton rushed into the room. She was a beautiful young woman with Titian locks tumbling about her shoulders. Her eyes were open wide, like a scared rabbit's, despite the heavy sedative that the town doctor had just administered.

'My God, Pam, he's going to come for me!' she almost shrieked. 'He's on a killing spree and it's me he wants to kill most.'

Pam put an arm about her friend's shoulders. 'No one wants to kill you, Evelyn!' she said firmly. 'Put that thought out of your mind right now.'

The banker's wife shook her head. 'No, you're wrong, Pam. He thinks I sent his brother to the gallows. Cash Meldrum wants me dead. I'm never going to set foot out of that door again.'

'Hush now, Evelyn,' said Pam. 'That scum raped you and deserved what he got. You hold your head up. I'm here to help you.'

Doc Munro put a hand on Pam's shoulder. 'Try

to persuade her to get out, Pam,' he whispered. 'She has to leave the house at least once every day. That's an important part of the treatment.'

Pam smoothed her friend's hair. 'Don't you worry none, Evelyn,' she said soothingly, 'I'm not going to let anyone harm you. And Cash Meldrum or no Cash Meldrum – you and I are going to go for a walk every day. I'm going to make you.'

Doc Munro smiled approvingly as Evelyn Bolton sobbed on Pam's shoulder. He picked up his bag and left silently.

Cash Meldrum raised his hands above his head and turned round slowly. Two men in range gear confronted him. They were about twenty yards apart and each one had a gun trained on him.

'That's it, Deacon,' said the one on the left, a man of about thirty-five, with dark eyes and a sadistic grin on his face. 'See you're about to have breakfast. Smells good.'

Cash Meldrum bobbed his head. 'There's enough for three, if you'd care to join me, friends.'

'Who said we're your friends!' barked the other, a lanky youth with an ugly scar on his face that seemed to fix his mouth in a permanent sneer. 'I don't like no bounty hunters,' he said, spitting contemptuously.

'Maybe if'n we sat down and ate together you'd find that we could be friends,' Meldrum replied. 'I'm afraid that I don't know your names. That kinda gives you boys an advantage.'

The scar-faced youth sneered, 'Yeah, and so do these guns. As for our names, they wouldn't mean nothing to you.' Then he glanced at his comrade. 'What d'you reckon we should do with him, Benson?'

The older man flashed an angry look at the youth, then he shrugged his shoulders and smiled resignedly. 'Well, now at least you know my name, Deacon. My young friend here is impetuous and sometimes a bit free with his mouth.' He snorted at his own humour. 'Which I guess is how he got his beauty mark.'

Despite himself, the youngster put a hand self-consciously to his face. 'The man who did that died a second after he did it,' he volunteered. Then, 'You know I don't like people talking about it, Benson.'

'A man shouldn't be judged by what he looks like,' said Cash Meldrum. 'He should be judged by what he does. Do you boys mind if'n I put my hands down now and get out of the water?'

The man called Benson clicked his tongue. 'Matter of fact we do mind, Deacon.' He knelt down by the fire where the fish was sizzling away in the pan. He prodded it and flicked it over. 'Sure smells good, but I don't think you're right: this little fish will never fill three growed up men with good appetites. I'd say there's only enough for two.' He grinned. 'Besides, me and my friend here

31

would like to see you swim a little.'

Meldrum looked down at the water lapping around his waist. 'Are you sure we can't be a bit less formal, fellers? I'm getting the impression that you don't wanna be friendly for some reason.'

'Damned right, we don't!' snapped scar face. 'You butchered kin o'mine.'

Meldrum frowned as if this news had deeply saddened him. 'Sorry to hear that. You gonna give me the name of your kin?'

The youth's face coloured as the knuckles of his gun-hand seemed to go white. 'You heard Benson, now swim, damn you, swim.'

Meldrum nodded and slowly stepped back-wards, gradually disappearing into the water as the river-bed sloped away. A moment later only his head remained above the surface as he trod water.

Benson laughed as he broke off a piece of fish and took a mouthful. 'Damn, that's tasty fish. Must be sweet water you're swimming in. Are you a good swimmer, Deacon?'

'Fair,' the bounty hunter replied.

'Then swim out a-ways,' Benson urged. 'I'd like to know if there's a current in that old river.'

'Then can I come out for a bite to eat?'

In answer the scar-faced youth let off a shot that zinged into the water alongside Cash's head. He needed no more urging, he sculled backwards, keeping an eye on the two men as he did so, his heart racing with anxiety as he half-expected death to come any second. The two men laughed cruelly.

'When I was a kid my pappy taught me to shoot at logs floating on the water,' cried Benson. And with a snap-shot from the hip he let off a shot that whistled perilously close to Cash's right ear.

Gulping a lungful of air, he bobbed underwater, somersaulted backwards and kicked for the bottom. A couple of hot bullets sizzled into the water above him, one skimming across his chest sending an agonizing pain searing through his brain. Involuntarily, precious air escaped from his lungs. But immediately his mind was focused on survival. He was aware that the moment he broke water bullets would be waiting to send him to Hell. And that was just someplace he had no intention of visiting yet. Swimming along the bottom with the current he fumbled in the silted river-bed and found a fist-sized stone. Then, reaching behind him, he unsheathed his Bowie knife. Clenching it between his teeth, he managed to peel his trousers off.

OK, you bastards! he thought, as he steadied himself, poised to kick for the surface. He held his discarded pants at arm's length and let the current take them. Then, as they gradually drifted away and upwards towards the surface, he grasped the Bowie knife in one hand and the stone in the other and kicked off from the bottom. Timing he knew was essential. As he rose through the water he was able to see, like a fish, the men on the bank.

His pants appeared on the surface about ten feet away and were immediately slashed by a fusillade of bullets. And in that instance Cash broke water, his right hand flashing back behind his head and then arcing forward to send the Bowie knife with unerring aim towards the now standing Benson. With a *kerchunking* noise it skewered his throat, causing his eyes to bulge instantly and a mouthful of fish to be forcefully ejected. He fell backwards across the fire, oblivious in death to the burning of his flesh.

The scar-faced youth had turned upon hearing the noise, giving Cash the moment's hesitation he had banked on. As the shocked kid recovered, snapping his gun round towards Cash, his mouth was still hanging open. Then the stone thudded into his face, smashing teeth and nasal bones and throwing him back on to the ground. With a few powerful strokes, Cash swam to the shore, leaped out and whipped his knife out of Benson's dead throat. He wheeled round just as the kid was feebly lifting his gun towards him. Again the bounty hunter's arm flashed back and forth, and the knife flew between them to spear the murderous youngster's heart. The body convulsed for a moment, then lay still.

In other circumstances he would have lashed their bodies to their mounts and ridden in with them to the nearest town. That was out of the question at this time, since he had other more pressing

34

plans. Having first retrieved his trousers and wrung the water out of them he applied a balm to the flesh wound on his chest, then he dug a shallow grave for the two would-be assassins. Despite their attempt to murder him he had no intention of leaving their bodies for the buzzards to pick clean. Apart from anything else, the less attention that was drawn to their demise the better, since they had clearly been sent by someone to wipe him out.

He laid coins over their eyes then covered them up with earth and rocks.

'Two more sinners for your consideration, Lord.' he mused, as he finished their makeshift graves, before applying himself to the unfinished task of fixing breakfast. Having briefly reconnoitered the area to ensure that he would be undisturbed, he set about catching himself another fish and then cooked it on a fresh fire. He whistled as he worked. Sometimes killing built up an extra strong appetite.

Despite the Deacon's swift reconnaissance he had failed to detect the heavily armed man who was watching him: the witness to the whole affair. From his hiding place up above in a small thicket of spruce, he looked down with interest as the bounty hunter ate heartily.

'Clever bastard, ain't you, Deacon?' the man whispered to himself. 'Always got a final trick up your sleeve. That's good, real good.'

He retraced his steps stealthily and made his way back to his own horse, his stomach rumbling after the smell of cooking. Like the Deacon, killing sometimes gave him an appetite too.

THREE

Wes Talbot walked purposefully along the board-walk towards Hiram G. Lanchester's Emporium, Hacksville's premier hardware and seed merchant-cum-general store. From previous experience he knew that he could order anything from a single nine-inch nail to a parasol of the latest Eastern design – at least according to Hiram. Wes had need of two purchases, one mundane, the other totally frivolous, though as yet unthought of. He would decide when something suitably frivolous caught his eye.

A bell jangled as he entered the store, a verita-ble cornucopia of items arranged in no obvious order. Jars of jam, onions and pickled eggs shared shelf-space with bails of wire, hurricane lanterns and rat repellent. Hooks were scattered over the walls, from which hung an old Army bugle (promi-nently marked 'not for sale'), assorted harnesses, ropes and 'dresses from Paris, France'. There was no system, either by category or simple alphabetical order; it was all assembled at the eccentric whim of the equally eccentric-looking Hiram G. Lanchester, a midget of a man, a trim five foot tall, but with an ego and entrepreneurial brain of gargantuan proportions. A former quartermaster in the US Army, he had never told anyone what the 'G' stood for, which in the bizarre way of the Southwest resulted in him being universally known as Hiram G.

'Judge Talbot, enter, peruse, be merry and financially unfettered,' he greeted, with a beaming grin and a twinkle in his eye that positively gleamed behind his half-moon spectacles. He was dressed in a starched-collared shirt with string tie and a leather apron. About his middle was strapped a thick belt from which hung a multitude of keys, and into which a Navy Colt .36 was prominently tucked. No one was sure whether it was loaded or not, for it had never been fired in anger. All one could say was that it appeared well tended and oiled, just like all the rifles, carbines and pistols that lay in the locked racks behind the main counter. As a gunsmith Hiram was certainly knowledgeable and careful as befitted a former US Army quartermaster.

'Be with you in a minute, Judge,' he added, as he pulled out a drawer of assorted ribbons and held them out for two female customers to inspect. Wes immediately recognized the bustles and the feather toques.

'Why Judge Talbot,' called out Betsy, the raven-haired younger singer, immediately crossing to meet him and linking her arm in his, then steering him back to the ribbon drawer. 'You've just what we need: a man's opinion.' She wrinkled her nose and winked. 'Which of these ribbons do you prefer? The plain coloured ones, the frilly red and black, or the plain white lace?'

Wes blustered, feeling confused.

'Betsy is talking garters, Judge,' Laura, the brunette, volunteered with a smile. 'She's moving in for the kill.'

Betsy cuffed her friend's arm. 'Don't listen none to her, Judge. I've met someone that's all.'

'Someone she wants to impress,' Laura went on.

Wes regained his composure. 'For you ma'am, I think maybe the plain white lace. That creates a good wholesome impression.'

Betsy pursed her lips and nodded. Then, as Hiram carefully wrapped the ribbons and added them to her other collection of purchases she said: 'For such a small town this far south I'd say it gets more than its fair share of excitement. That poor man burned alive in that fire.'

'Wasn't he the sheriff you were talking to when we came in on the stage?' Laura asked.

Wes nodded. 'Sheriff Henry Logan, yes, ma'am. He was a good man and a fine sheriff.'

Hiram G. Lanchester sniffed, as if expressing dry-eyed but choked sadness. 'A good lawman, but now we've no law here.'

'But the Judge here is the law, isn't that right, Judge?' Betsy asked.

Wes shook his head. 'I dispense the law, ma'am, but I wouldn't say that I was the law. And Hiram here is right: the town is unprotected at the moment. It needs a new lawman.'

The two ladies collected their purchases and made their way to the door. Before leaving, Betsy turned and smiled. 'Well, we're pretty good at getting men to volunteer, Judge. Maybe we'll just find you a lawman.' And giggling girlishly they left the store.

Hiram G grinned after them. 'That young lady Betsy, didn't waste any time in Hacksville,' he announced. 'Been here a day and already she's had old Ben Taverner, the owner of the Jagged J ranch, rumbling publicly about proposing.'

Wes laughed, fully understanding the significance of the garter ribbons. But a glance at the large clock ticking away above the counter stimulated him to speed up his shopping. He ordered a box of cigars, a bottle of ink, a tin of boot polish and a new ledger. Then, his mind moved to matters more frivolous, and almost as an afterthought he ordered a good length of the red and black frilly garter ribbon.

Hiram G. Lanchester's eyes twinkled behind his spectacles, but he said not a word as he measured and cut a good length.

*

The garters looked handsome on each shapely thigh scissored round Wes Talbot. And as he and Pam finished their passionate love-making and rolled apart to stare breathlessly up at the ceiling, Wes silently thanked Betsy for giving him the idea of a gift.

He and Pam had been lovers for about six months, snatching odd hours together whenever he came to Hacksville. Sometimes they met in Pam's house when they could be assured that her father would be kept at the *Chronicle* office for a long time, or, like now, they would share the large bed in Wes's room at the Hacksville Grand Hotel.

Pam turned to face him, naked except for the wisps of black and red ribbon about her thighs. 'You're a wicked man, Judge Talbot,' she said, mock accusingly.

'You mean I'm not behaving like a judge ought to!' He drew her to him and kissed her nose. 'I'm afraid that I'd have to disagree, Pam. I'm passionate about the truth, and the truth is that I'm passionate about you, so logically my motives, actions and deeds must all be truthful and honourable.'

Pam stroked his side with her gartered thigh. 'You're too clever for your own good, Mister Judge. And I still think you're just a wicked man who takes a pleasure in sinning.'

'I'm a man of flesh and blood, Pam. Just that. And you're the most attractive woman since Eve.'

Pam laughed and put a finger to her pouting lips. 'Which means that I'm just a seductress. A sinful woman.'

Wes kissed her again. 'You're a mite frisky, I admit, but I reckon you don't have a proper sin in your soul. What we're doing isn't sinning, in my opinion.' Then his face grew more serious. 'As a matter of fact, I think that it's about time that we made all this – legal! What say I have a word with Phin as soon as possible? Do it properly and ask him for your hand?'

She nodded then kissed him passionately. 'But not today, Wes. Wait until tomorrow. After the funeral.'

Wes nodded agreement. 'I understand, Pam. It kinda makes you feel guilty, doesn't it? Us so happy, making love, making plans for the future, when poor Henry is lying there dead.'

'I hate that Cash Meldrum,' Pam whispered. 'Just like I hate his brother for what he did to Evelyn.' She looked up and peered questioningly into his eyes. 'What makes men so evil that they can do things like that, Wes? What makes them believe they can take what they want, kill people?'

Wes shook his head. 'Who knows what turns someone bad. Some are born that way, I guess.' He squeezed her reassuringly. 'But he'll be brought to justice, Pam, and if he's found guilty in my court,

I'll sentence him appropriately. And if that means he's found guilty of murder, then I'll sentence him to be hanged, just like his brother.'

The tone of his voice made her feel easier. He was so strong, so sure of himself. 'You've got a strong sense of justice, haven't you, Wes?'

'It's the only hope for this country, Pam. We have to have men who can enforce the law and men who can dispense justice. I was a lawman like Henry Logan before I studied jurisprudence and became a judge. The law is there to protect everyone. Justice is everything in my opinion, Pam.'

'Aren't you frightened that he might come after you?' Her eyes registered fear, concern for him.

He smiled down at her and kissed the corner of her mouth. 'I can take care of myself, my darling. And I can look after you.'

'Poor Evelyn,' said Pam. 'I don't know if Dexter Bolton can do the same for her.' And then she started and sat up in bed. 'My God, Wes. Evelyn! I'm supposed to be going with her to the bank, with Dexter's lunch. I promised.'

And before he could stop her she was dressing and preparing to leave.

'I think I'll go and see Phin now,' he said, as she kissed him goodbye.

But she was preoccupied now. 'Fine, tell him I'll be in before three o'clock. Once I've taken Evelyn back home.'

*

43

Evelyn had packed a hamper for Dexter, just as usual, but was in a high state of anxiety when Pam unlocked the door in answer to the pre-arranged knock on the kitchen window. 'I don't know if I can face this, Pam,' the banker's wife whispered, biting her lower lip.

'Of course you can, Evelyn,' replied Pam firmly, picking up the hamper in one hand and linking arms with her friend as she steered her towards the door. 'We can't let poor old Dexter starve, can we?'

The main street was busy with people going to and from lunch in the several eating establishments dotted around town. Riders ambled about their business and a couple of urchins ran in pursuit, scooping up the rich damp droppings in buckets to sell to the local livery.

The two women began to cross the street when a high-pitched whistle made them look towards a heavily laden buckboard being hauled up the road by a mule. A couple of horses were tethered to the back and trotted along behind. The driver was a brawny, heavily jowled teamster with a red handle-bar moustache and a mind-your-own business kind of face. He barely acknowledged the two women as they halted in their tracks and allowed the buckboard to rumble by them. It was the young man sitting on the tarpaulin load in the back who had whistled at them and who was now grinning at them with an expression that seemed both lascivious and insolent. His greasy yellow hair hung lankly about his shoulders and he twiddled a strand and put the end in his mouth. 'Good day, ladies,' he called. 'Join me for a drink later? I've got money.'

'Ignore him, Evelyn,' Pam said, as her friend stiffened in her tracks. And she hustled her on as the buckboard passed. 'He's just a drifter, pay him no mind.'

'I want to go back, Pam,' Evelyn whispered, her voice trembling. 'I can't do this.'

But Pam would not hear of it. With her arm tightly locked in her friend's she guided her across the street on to the opposite boardwalk and up towards the bank.

Wes Talbot looked out of the *Hacksville Chronicle* office window and smiled at the sight of the two women walking away in the other direction. He had seen their brief encounter with the youth in the buckboard and realized that he had obviously said something that had rattled Evelyn. Pam had clearly handled the situation, as he knew she would handle any awkward customer.

'So what did you want me for, Wes?' asked Phin Bradley from behind him. Wes turned and smiled uncertainly at the newspaperman, who was sitting at his desk, stuffing tobacco into his large pipe. 'Business or pleasure?'

'It's sort of personal business,' said Wes, regarding Tom Granville, the *Hacksville Chronicle* general dogsbody hovering in the back of the office.

Phin chuckled as he shouted through for Tom to take a break and fetch a couple of soda pops from Hiram G.'s Emporium. Then a moment later, once they were alone again, he struck a light to his pipe and started producing plumes of smoke. His eyes twinkled. 'I've been expecting you to call on me for some time,' he said, opening the conversation.

Wes flushed slightly and a hand went to loosen his tie. 'It's about Pam and me.' He shuffled his feet, feeling more nervous than he had done in years. Part of him felt as if he'd rather face down a double murderer in his court than stand here and ask Phin Bradley for his daughter's hand. He turned and looked out of the window, up the street towards the bank, outside which the buckboard had been pulled up.

'What about you and Pam?' Phin prompted him.

But Wes was now watching the two men. The driver had unhitched the mule and was leading it away, while the younger man was stripping back the tarpaulin. A flame appeared at his hand and a moment later smoke and flames were rising from the back of the buckboard. Thick black smoke that was soon drifting across the street.

'Something's wrong, Phin!' Wes gasped. He charged out of the door.

But as he hit the boardwalk there came a terrific explosion from the middle of the street.

'That was dynamite!' exclaimed Phin, a couple of paces behind Wes.

And then out from five side-streets galloped men on horses, guns blazing. In moments they had converged upon the smoke-screened bank and three of them dismounted and rushed inside, while two mounted guard behind the buckboard, joined by the young man from the buckboard and the driver, both now mounted on the spare unsaddled horses. Together they started firing warning shots at anyone they saw. From self-preservation all the townsfolk had deserted the streets, heading for cover.

Wes drew his Remington-Elliot pepperbox and advanced slowly up the street.

'You damned fool, don't go near them,' Phin said, trying to grasp Wes's sleeve. 'You want to get your head shot off? That's a bank robbery.'

Wes firmly removed the newspaperman's hand. 'I can see that,' he hissed. 'And Pam has just gone in there with Evelyn Bolton.'

Phin's face went pale. 'But you've only got a derringer pepperbox. What good is that against heavily armed men?'

Wes knew he was right, but his woman was in the bank, in danger at that very moment. He wasn't sure if he was going to try to do anything more than get close so that he could at least have a chance of protecting her.

He had just advanced to the cover of a wood

pillar when suddenly, from across the street came a string of shots aimed at the shadowy figures behind the smokescreen. Wes darted a glance over and saw Hiram G. Lanchester sheltering in his doorway, a Volcanic lever action carbine at his shoulder. The little man dodged back inside as a couple of bullets gouged out splinters close to his head, then a moment later he poked the carbine round again and swiftly levered off three rounds. This time one of them found a target, and one of the men on horseback clutched his chest and fell backwards off his horse as the .38 bored through his heart. Immediately, a fusillade of shots was directed at Hiram, and Wes watched in helpless horror as one bullet struck the little storekeeper in the thigh and he fell backwards into his shop, the carbine falling from his hands as he writhed in agony.

Then one of the men was galloping down the street, suddenly sliding over the saddle, clinging on with one leg hooked over so that he was sheltered by the body of his horse. In his hand a stick of dynamite fizzed and smoked.

'Wes, he's going to get Hiram!' cried Phin.

And as the rider drew level with Wes, he drew back his arm to hurl the dynamite under the horse's neck at the open door of the store.

Wes's derringer barked once, shattering the outlaw's knee causing him to fall with a scream under the horse's hooves. Two seconds later, before he had time to react in any way other than to moan, the dynamite exploded and literally blew him to pieces.

Before the dust cloud settled, Wes was running across the street towards the wounded Hiram.

'Wes, watch out!' cried Phin.

Spinning round, he heard, then saw the group of riders bearing down on him. Their guns were firing indiscriminately, as if to discourage any further resistance on the part of the townsfolk. Wes hurled his derringer aside and dived for the boardwalk, rolling when he landed to gather up Hiram's Volcanic repeater. Straightening up with the carbine at his shoulder he aimed to dish out some justice to the escaping bank robbers.

But he heard Dexter Bolton's voice scream at him from the direction of the bank, 'Don't shoot! For Gawd's sake, don't anyone shoot!'

As they passed at speed, Wes saw the reason why. The bodies of two women were hanging across the necks of two saddle-less horses, their legs kicking madly while the riders ruthlessly yet skilfully spurred their mounts onwards. Wes dodged inside as a bullet zinged in his direction. A moment later he had the Volcanic back at his shoulder, drawing a bead on the outlaw with the lank blond hair. His finger was about to squeeze the trigger when Phin cried out, 'It's Pam!'

Wes pulled the carbine upwards, letting the bullet discharge skywards. He cursed, for he had missed his opportunity to send the man to Hell. Yet he had no choice. There was no way he was going to risk hitting Evelyn Bolton or Pam, the woman he loved.

As the outlaws galloped unhindered out of town the screams of the two women echoed in his ears and he felt sick and helpless.

FOUR

The town was in turmoil. As soon as the thieves had left town, people started leaving their shelter, drifting out into the main street. There were two craters gouged out by the dynamite explosions, several shot-up shop-fronts, a busted-open bank, one wounded storekeeper, the corpse of a bank robber and an assortment of body parts peppered across the street. Of these, only the wounded Hiram G. Lanchester received any immediate attention as a crowd formed outside the bank.

'What d'you reckon we oughta do, Dexter?' called out a man in shirt-sleeves and a bowler hat, who had been depositing his takings when the bank had been hit.

'Let's get up a posse!' shouted someone from the crowd.

'Call the army!' cried another.

'What sorta town is this with no lawman.'

There were lots of cussings and sage advisings,

51

but it was essentially a leaderless crowd. Ordinarily the by and large law-abiding citizens of Hacksville had expected Henry Logan to make all the decisions about peacekeeping. They had grown used to him and his famous Le Mat ten-shooter to keep trouble away from Hacksville. The fact that the town sheriff was dead and not yet buried seemed to pass by a lot of people. In this land of sudden death there was almost an atmosphere of disdain about him having been negligent enough to get himself killed, thereby leaving the town unprotected.

Dexter Bolton was ashen faced and stunned, barely able to talk, let alone offer suggestions. 'They . . . they've taken my Evie!' was all he could say.

Just then a group of six men rode up from the stockyard at the east of the town. The leader, a stocky, ruddy-faced man dressed in his best suit, boots and Stetson dismounted and questioned the banker about all the noise they'd heard.

'The bastards!' he spat. 'My boys'll get 'em,' he announced. He signalled to a tall, red-haired rider. 'You heard all that, Red?' And when the ranch foreman nodded determinedly, Ben Taverner, the owner of the Jagged J, a man used to command, issued the order, 'Then go get 'em.'

The five cowboys took off at speed, oblivious to the warnings of caution from some of the older men present.

'Where are those hotheads going?' Wes called, pushing his way through the crowd, as he and Phin helped the wounded Hiram G. towards Doc Munro's surgery.

'It's a posse,' Dexter explained. 'I . . . I guess I ought to be with them. They . . . they've got my Evie,' he added helplessly.

'Don't worry, my boys will soon bring them in,' said Ben Taverner confidently. 'They're good men.'

'They're damned fools!' said Wes, through gritted teeth. 'Those men have taken two women hostage, which means they aren't playing some game. They could make matters ten times worse.'

The rancher drew himself up to his full height, which was about a head shorter than Wes. 'I don't much like your tone – whoever you are!' Then before Wes could reply, he nodded to Phin and Hiram. 'You want to get that leg patched up, Hiram.' With no more ado he straightened his Stetson and made a way through the crowd towards the Lucky Belle Saloon. And as if that was a signal, the crowd began to disperse away from the bank.

'Pompous clown!' said Phin dismissively, his face as worried and pale as the banker's. 'What d'you think we should do, Wes?'

Wes looked concernedly at the agony-racked storekeeper between them. 'Like the man says, get Hiram patched up first, then we need to think carefully about what we do. That was a well-planned robbery, but it was badly botched. They lost two men and they've taken two women hostage.'

'Just why the hell would they do that, Wes?' asked Dexter. 'It doesn't make sense.'

Hiram G. Lanchester had been clenching his teeth in pain, but now he let out a gasp, followed by a string of invectives fit to make a mule-skinner blush. 'An' it don't make sense to let me bleed to death on the street here neither! Just get me to the sawbones, then you can have a chin-wag.'

The posse returned within the hour. Two of the men were riding on one horse and another had a bandanna tied round his arm, a blood-soaked sleeve telling its own tale.

'The clever scum were waiting for us as we went into Pintos Canyon,' explained Red O'Leary, the lanky foreman of the Jagged J ranch, as he recounted their chase to his boss Ben Taverner, in the Lucky Belle saloon where an eager crowd had already gathered round the bar. The rancher's cheeks were flushed and, despite the drama of the morning and the wounding of one of his men, he looked distinctly pleased with himself. The reason for his good humour, Betsy Manion, was standing beside him, her slim waist encircled by his arm. She was at least fifteen years younger than him and a good two inches taller, but her smile was enchanting as she darted admiring glances first at him then at the brand new engagement ring he had just given her. A little to the side of them, her eyes ever flashing enviously at the ring, stood her friend Laura.

'They had us in a crossfire from up above,' Red went on. 'Little Steve lost his mount and Jed caught one in the arm.'

'I shoulda come with you,' Ben Taverner announced, perhaps more loudly than was necessary. He was determined to let his new fiancée know that he was the most powerful man around these parts. 'Tactics was needed to outsmart those jaspers.' He turned and patted Betsy's hand reassuringly. 'Don't let any of this worry you, honey. I'm going to look after you. And the first thing I'm going to show you is how we deal with bank robbers round here. I'm going to—'

'You're going to do nothing!' came an authoritative voice from the batwing doors of the saloon. Wes, Dexter and Phin had just come in, with Hiram G. Lanchester hobbling behind them on crutches. 'I'd say that you'd done quite enough damage already,' said Wes.

Ben Taverner's jaw muscles tightened. 'Who the hell are you to go spouting at me like that?' he barked.

But it was Betsy who supplied the answer. She beamed at Wes. 'Why Judge Talbot,' she said 'This is my fiancé, Ben Taverner. He owns the Jagged J ranch, if you didn't know.'

The two men looked a tad embarrassed at Betsy's smiling introduction. Then the rancher recovered himself. 'Judge, eh? Well as I was about to tell everyone here, I'm prepared to send another posse, a bigger better prepared one this time, into the Pintos to get those robbers.'

'And I say you'll do no such thing. You have no authority to form a posse.' And as the rancher flustered and blustered, searching for words that wouldn't come, Wes went on, 'I'm the judge on this circuit and in the absence of a duly appointed town sheriff, I am empowered by law to take over responsibility.'

Dexter Bolton was no longer ashen-faced, but his voice still shook. 'What do you propose, Wes? We have to do something about the bank's money.' Then he hung his head limply. 'And we have to do something about Evie.'

'And Pam!' added Phin forcefully. 'Remember they've got my Pam too, for God's sake.'

Hiram thumped a crutch on the floor to draw attention. 'I can supply guns,' he offered.

Wes shook his head. 'There will be no more posses going into the Pintos Canyon.'

A chorus of disapproval and disbelief ran round the saloon. Wes held up his hands. 'This town is unprotected. At the moment anyone could hit us again. We need to fortify the town, post guards and appoint a deputy sheriff.'

At this a murmur of approval ran around the room.

'That makes sense,' said Hiram.

Phin's pipe had gone cold and he clenched the mouthpiece between his teeth. 'All well and good, but what about the hostages? In case you had forgotten – *Judge* – Pam and Evelyn are out there somewhere right now.'

'I'm going to contact the military,' Wes replied. Turning to Phin and the others, his steely look told them that this was not the place to argue with him.

'In the meanwhile,' he went on, 'we need to appoint a deputy sheriff. Anyone here ever had any law experience?'

Ben Taverner clapped his foreman's shoulder. 'Red was a deputy constable in a town on the Panhandle a few years back. He'd be a good choice – and I'd back him with more of my boys.' He looked defiantly at Wes. 'How would that suit you for fortifying the town, Judge?'

Red O'Leary looked gratefully at his boss, then turned to Wes. 'I'm willing if that suits you, Judge.'

Wes nodded. 'Just so long as we understand one thing: you're appointed to guard this town, not to authorize or sanction any more posses.'

Ben Taverner answered for his foreman. 'We'll do what needs to be done Talbot.' Then he smiled indulgently at the lovely Betsy, glad to have regained his dignity and standing as a man of power in the town. Her look of admiration broadened his smile and brought more colour to his ruddy cheeks.

Wes duly swore Red O'Leary into office in front of the assembled saloon crowd. Then he led Phin, Hiram and Dexter out as Ben Taverner ordered drinks for all present to toast the appointment of his foreman – and to celebrate his forthcoming marriage to Betsy Manion.

Laura Green, Betsy's friend and fellow adventurer, put her arm through Red's and raised a glass to him. 'How about a song, pretty lady?' Red asked her. Laura sipped her drink, squeezed his arm then disengaged herself as she headed for the small dais while the crowd cheered and the piano player struck up a tune. She turned and smiled at Betsy, and they exchanged glances, the meaning of which they both understood. Red O'Leary was not a bad-looking guy. Maybe they were both about to strike lucky.

Phin Bradley smoked furiously as he paced up and down the office of the *Hacksville Chronicle*. Dexter Bolton and Hiram were sitting in the plush leather armchairs reserved for clients while Wes Talbot stood looking out the window at the main street, where Zach Lewis, the town undertaker and his two sons, all dressed in dirty leather aprons went about scattering swarms of blowflies as they picked up body parts and dumped them unceremoniously in a rough coffin on a handcart. The corpse of the other bank thief they had already loaded into an adjoining lidless coffin. A group of urchins danced amid them, unperturbed by the sight, almost revelling in the gruesome excitement that the robbery had brought to the mundane life of Hacksville.

Finally, in exasperation, Phin took his pipe out of his mouth and thundered, 'Damn it Wes, when in tarnation are you going to tell us what's going on!'

Wes turned round and nodded. He was himself feeling deeply unsettled, fearful for Pam's safety, yet he knew that any moves had to be carefully considered. There was no way he planned on putting Pam or Evelyn at any more risk than they already were. 'I'm working out how we can save them, Phin.'

'So what was all that about getting the military?' Phin asked. 'You know damned well that it'll take two days at least before we can get any kind of response from them.'

'That's what I figured,' Wes replied.

'Then why won't you let us send in a posse?' Dexter asked.

Phin shook his head and folded his muscular forearms in despair. 'You were a lawman before you became a judge, why didn't you appoint yourself as sheriff and take a posse in? You know how to organize one and the town would back you.'

Wes sighed. 'Because no posse would be allowed to get near. You heard how those boys were cut down. If that gang had wanted to they could have finished them all off just like that,' he said, snapping his fingers for emphasis. 'Don't you see that they let them go as a warning? Anyone going in there with a star would be the first to be wiped out. I'm betting those guys have got lookouts tucked away at all the right bushwhacking points.'

Hiram produced a snuff box and took a hefty sniff up each nostril. 'I think I see what your game plan is.'

Phin absent-mindedly struck a match and puffed his pipe into action. 'Blasted if I do.'

Wes smiled without humour. 'Only a lone agent can do this, Phin. Not a judge, sheriff or any kind of lawman. Only an outlaw, someone on the wrong side of the law like them will have a chance of getting into the Pintos.'

Realization dawned. 'So that's why you appointed Red O'Leary and let that idiot Ben Taverner think that he's doing something useful!' exclaimed Phin. 'That'll keep them all out of the way.'

'And the military not coming for two days ought to give this outlaw, whoever he is, a head start,' added Dexter.

'That's right,' said Wes. 'But this has got to be kept secret from everyone in town. I'm going in there alone, but I need some help.'

'I'll gear you up,' Hiram G. Lanchester offered. 'Duds, irons. You can shoot, I guess.' He pursed his lips, as if assessing Wes's size for a new suit. 'I'm guessing Navy Colts should do you.'

Wes nodded. 'Spot on, Hiram. But I have my own in my room. A Winchester wouldn't go amiss though.'

'You can take my gelded bay,' Dexter offered. 'Faster than I've ever needed, but well trained.'

Phin tapped his teeth with the mouthpiece of his pipe. 'So how soon will you go?'

'As soon as possible. This afternoon, just as soon as I change and take on my new identity.' He frowned. 'It's a pity that the sheriff's office was blown up. Henry Logan's wanted posters would have come in most handy right now.'

The ghost of a smile hovered across Phin Bradley's lips. 'Who do you think printed them?' he asked, reaching into a drawer and removing a wad of wanted posters. He spread them out on the desk. 'Take your pick.'

The four men scrutinized the pictures of the assorted villains, murderers and conmen. At last, Wes selected one bearing the name 'Diamond Jim Crane – Wanted for Murder, Theft and Rape.' Below it was a short listing of his crimes, then a reward offer of $1,000. The picture was not a million miles from Wes in appearance and build, except that he was a blond-haired charmer who clearly favoured flashy waistcoats and fine shirts.

'I've got peroxide at the Emporium,' Hiram offered. 'We can bleach your hair and dandy you up a bit, but do you think you can act the role?'

Wes nodded. 'In my sheriff days I lived around a heap of characters like this and I reckon I know enough tricks with paste-boards to hold my own in a poker game.'

And indeed, a couple of hours later, in the back room of the Emporium the three townsmen looked admiringly at the new incarnation of Diamond Jim Crane, blond-haired dude, gambler and wanted desperado. Wishing him luck, they watched him exit the town on Dexter's gelded bay, armed to the teeth with Hiram's best Winchester, specially prepared according to Wes's specifications, and as much well-wishing as they could shower on him.

'Guess he never figured he'd end up a judge on the run,' Hiram G said.

The other two men said nothing. They knew only too well that his chances of success were pretty miserable.

With his hat pulled down low, Wes let the bay amble slowly along the street, seemingly ignoring the other riders coming and going to town. So deep in thought was he that he neither noticed nor was noticed by the man in black who passed him on his way into town.

The Deacon rode on up the main street and hitched his horse outside the Lucky Belle Saloon. He was thirsty for both drink and information, a combination that he knew often went hand in hand. He felt in his pocket as he opened the batwing doors and crossed to the bar where a couple of bar-bums had turned to eye him with curiosity and hope. Their eyes gleamed when they saw him draw out a couple of silver dollars and slam them on the counter.

Cash smiled as he saw the regulars edge towards him. He smiled inwardly, sure that he was about to slake his thirst for both things.

FIVE

The sun was beginning its descent from an azure sky by the time Wes Talbot, in his new persona of Diamond Jim Crane entered Pintos Canyon. It was a long meandering track bound on either side by red rock walls, in the parched crevices of which cacti and other self-sewn, water-preserving vegetation grew sparsely and mysteriously. Gigantic boulders and countless rock falls had created a perfect terrain for a man to hide in and pick off anyone who came nosing along the trail.

With his hat pulled down low to give the impression of near somnolence as he lumbered along on Dexter's bay, Wes's eyes darted hither and thither exploring the route ahead. When he had gone about quarter of a mile he stopped and deliberately pulled out his Winchester and tied a handkerchief to the end of the barrel. Then even more deliberately he drew out a cheroot and struck a light. Once he had it lit and going to his satisfaction, he hoisted the Winchester against his shoulder and then urged the bay onwards, the handkerchief hanging prominently from the barrel as a flag of truce.

The trail narrowed further and zigzagged back and forth, making his progress slow and mighty vulnerable to any observer who might happen to be watching from the rocks above. And that, of course, was precisely what he wanted, which is why he began singing in a none-too tuneful manner an old Texas ditty about the daddy of all longhorns. Inevitably, his theatrically dulcet tones echoed about the canyon walls.

From behind a tangle of scrub on a ledge about thirty yards ahead of him he saw a man emerge with a rifle trained on him. Wes pretended not to notice him and let the bay saunter on.

'Cut that damned caterwauling and hold it right there!' barked the man. 'Unless you aim to get yourself ventilated,' he sneered. 'Kinda stupid, ain't you, to go announcing your arrival like that?'

Wes lifted his head slowly and grinned up at the man, whom he recognized as the driver of the buckboard that he had seen earlier that day. He was a stocky none-too-clever-looking man with a red handlebar moustache and a wrinkled complexion that told of having spent a considerable number of years in the open. 'I resent being called stupid, mister,' Wes said, still grinning, 'especially when I've gone to such pains to give you advance warning of my coming.' He waggled his Winchester to emphasize the handkerchief. 'And my white flag oughta tell you that I'm a friend.'

The man lowered his rifle a touch as he took in Wes's appearance, especially the two tied-down holsters with the ivory handles of twin Navy Colts protruding. A brow muscle twitched as if indicating that he was making a difficult decision. 'Didn't mean any offence, stranger. But this is Rough Rider land, and my boss don't like any strangers nosing around.' His lips parted in a yellow-toothed grin. 'We already had to dissuade unwelcome visitors from trespassing earlier on. Now what did you say your name was?'

Wes shook his head and chewed reflectively on his smoking cheroot. 'I didn't say, friend. And I won't while-ever you have that cannon pointed in my direction.'

Again a muscle twitched, this time at the side of the man's mouth, making the red moustache quiver uncertainly. 'Maybe I'll take those guns off you. The boss don't let anyone pass with hardware.' Then he smiled and his eyes gave away the lie that he was about to utter. 'My pard has had a rifle pointed at your back for the last five minutes. Now shuck those guns and gimme your name!'

But Wes didn't move a muscle. Instead, he took the cheroot out of his mouth and scrutinized the glowing tip. 'You a gambling man, my friend?'

Red moustache eyed him quizzically.

'Because if you are, I'm willing to bet that you're out here on your own.' He rolled the cheroot between his fingers, then suddenly flicked it upwards towards the rifleman, whose eyes reflexively followed the arc of the cigar. When he recovered himself a split second later he found himself looking at the barrel of a Navy Colt that seemed to have appeared in Wes's hand. He cursed in wide-eyed horror, aware that if he chose, Wes could probably blast him to hell before he could get a bead on him again with his rifle.

'You see, friend,' Wes went on, the grin having returned to his face, 'I am a betting man, and I guess I win. There's no one at my back. Now put down that cannon, like I asked nicely.' When the man complied he holstered his weapon. 'Now I'm willing to give you my name – after I hear yours.'

'They call me Wheeler,' the man replied, his face having visibly paled.

'And you're with the Rough Riders?'

'I'm the teamster for 'em.'

'I've heard it's a good outfit to work for,' Wes said. 'That's why I've been flying this flag o' peace. I came through a town a few miles back and I guess you boys paid them a visit today. I hear they're planning to plant two of your boys.'

Wheeler nodded dispassionately, as if the loss of two members of the gang was of little importance. So much for honour among thieves, Wes thought, with a surge of disgust.

'They sent a posse after us and we shied them off. They won't risk coming this far into the Pintos again without a lot of thought – or a lot of men.'

That was just as Wes had thought. And his impression of the Pintos was that a small army could easily lose itself in there. Which was why they had left Wheeler, probably an expendable member of the gang, to guard the main way in. If it had been a posse rather than a lone man he reckoned that he wouldn't have revealed himself, but would have somehow signalled to someone further along the way.

'Well there's just me – Diamond Jim Crane – come to see about joining you boys,' Wes announced. 'Texas has lately gotten a bit too hot for my liking.'

At mention of the name Wheeler's eyes registered recognition and a tinge of fear. Clearly the reputation of Diamond Jim had gone far. Gambler, thief and killing machine, Wes was aware that he had chosen a name that could be considered an asset to such men as rode with the Rough Riders. 'The boss will want you to leave your hardware with me,' Wheeler said.

Diamond Jim shook his head. 'No one takes my weapons, Wheeler. Now point me in the right direction.'

A few moments later, he was ambling along the trail with his Winchester flagpole held vertically in front of him. He had again adopted his air of nonchalance, yet he was in reality entirely vigilant. Before he had left Hiram G. Lanchester's Emporium he had selected the Winchester very carefully, partly because he liked its balance, but also because of its highly polished breech, which he had asked Hiram to shine to mirror brilliance. As he rode, he kept an eye on Wheeler's crow's nest hiding-place. And, as if on cue, he caught the reflection of a mirror being flashed. About quarter of a mile further along the undulating trail he saw a flicker from rocks, undoubtedly from the stock of another rifle lying in wait. He smiled to himself. He had been right: the Rough Riders had strung out a series of lookouts just in case another posse came in force.

Ned Slade was lying on his belly behind a pile of rocks, his rifle protruding through a gap to cover the trail. He grinned as he saw the mirror signal from Wheeler, then he watched the lone rider advance along the trail on the bay, a white flag hanging from his rifle. As the man drew slowly nearer he observed that not only did he have a rifle, but he was wearing his guns, two of them.

'The boss isn't going to be happy with you, Wheeler boy,' he mused. He ran his fingers through his lank yellow hair then slid his hat on and shuffled his way backwards, so that he could get into a crouching position unobserved from the trail below. 'Well, I ain't gonna let him slip through with all that hardware,' he whispered to himself, and made his way sidewards, so that he would be able to get the jump on the rider as the trail snaked round the jutting outcrop of rock that he had been resting atop.

He heard the clip-clop of hooves approach and steadied himself, ready to spring out and get the drop on the rider. If the stranger reacted, well, that would be too bad for him. Maybe he'd just have to kill him and take those guns of his for himself. Besides, he thought with another grin, he liked killing.

The bay's head appeared round the corner. He saw the white flag hanging from the rifle, just as he prepared to leap to his feet. And a moment later the whole horse came into view, as did the rifle stuck in the top of its scabbard – but there was no rider.

What the—? he mouthed silently.

Then he heard the ratchet of a Navy Colt hammer being drawn back, and felt the cold steel of a barrel being pressed to the side of his temple. 'Not a sound, friend,' he heard a calm voice urge. 'Now lay the rifle down and shuck your weapon.'

Slade let out a snort-like laugh. 'Ha! Made a monkey outa me, didn't you, stranger! You do the same to old Wheeler?'

Wes kicked the guns aside then removed his revolver from the younger man's temple. 'He kindly let me pass, just like you're going to,' he said. He pointed at the lengthening late afternoon shadows. 'If you're gonna hide from a man, make sure you dub down the shine from your rifle, and hide yourself where your shadow ain't gonna give you away.'

Ned Slade turned with a grin to face the man who had bettered him. 'Pretty clever, mister. You've been about a bit, I guess. Have to admit that was a fancy trick you pulled on me. My name's Slade, Ned Slade, what about your'n?'

'I'm called Diamond Jim Crane,' Wes said, now fully recognizing the man as the one who had carried off Pam earlier that day. His hand tightened on the butt of his gun, as he felt an urge to pistol-whip this young cur. But he forced the thought away immediately. He was here to rescue the two women and that meant that he had to carry off his part and gain access to the Rough Riders' camp, wherever it was. Dealing with this young bastard might give him satisfaction, but it wouldn't do a scrap of good for Pam or Evelyn. He forced a smile to his lips, then, 'I'm looking to spend a bit of time with the Rough Riders.'

Slade's grin spread further across his face. 'That'll be up to the boss, o' course. But I reckon he'll jump at having a famous killer like you join up. I hear tell you've got notches on notches.'

Wes could see the enthusiasm on the younger man's face. He couldn't have been much more than about twenty-one, but he had the unsavoury

71

look of one who had killed and who probably revelled in killing. 'I take care of myself,' Wes replied. 'And those I like. But anyone who crosses me—' He left the end of the sentence unspoken, the meaning all too clear.

Slade grinned. 'Well, Diamond Jim, if'n you'll let me get my irons I'll take you into Rough Valley, our very own town. It takes a deal of finding, so it's better if I take you in. Besides,' he added, 'it'll save you having to tangle with Webster up the trail. I'd sure hate to see you hurt his feelings like you did with Wheeler and me.'

Slade had been speaking the truth when he said it was difficult to find. The trail broke into a multitude of different directions, some leading into box canyons, others veering away in a veritable maze of possibilities. But after about half an hour of picking their way through the network of undulating trails the way opened into a small valley. Lush grass grew on the valley floor and some distance away they saw what almost amounted to a small ranch. On a small rise there stood a main two-storeyed house built of adobe and timber, complete with veranda and steps. Below it there was a sort of barn and a cluster of cruder lean-to type huts and sheds. A fair number of Brahman and Charolais cattle were grazing in a penned-off field while a full corral of cow ponies and a number of men moving around like ants proclaimed the fact that this was essentially a working ranch.

'Rough Valley, our own home sweet home,' Slade announced, as he began the descent. They were greeted warily by several men as they made their way into the heart of the ranch.

They hitched their mounts at a pole outside a low squat building, from whence came the noise of cheering and jeering men and the howls and yowls of enraged animals.

'The boys'll be having some fun in the saloon,' Slade volunteered in answer to Wes's raised eyebrows. 'Care for a drink?'

Wes nodded and the two of them entered the building, taking a moment or two to accustom their eyes to the smoky, shadowy interior. About twenty men were smoking and drinking as they either stood by a rough bar, consisting of a couple of planks supported on barrels, or hung over the sides of a sunken ring in the centre of the dirt floor room. It was from thence that the noise of fighting animals came.

'Gonzalez, our saloon-keeper, organizes little entertainments,' Slade explained. 'The boys like to bet. Fancy a flutter, Diamond Jim?'

Wes looked into the pit and saw a mass of blood, teeth and flying fur. A dog and a coyote were locked in a death battle, urged on by the blood-crazed punters. 'The coyote will win,' he announced. 'Hardly worth the bet.'

Slade grinned. 'Have a drink then?'

But, as he turned to the bar, a large man with a patch over his left eye and two ruffianly looking rangemen broke away from the crowd. 'Why have you left your post, Slade?' the big man asked.

'I brought Diamond Jim Crane in to see the boss,' Slade replied. And as a gathering group fell in around them he fleetingly explained how Wes had outsmarted both Wheeler and himself. 'Now I'm gonna get us a drink,' he said.

The big man hooked his thumbs in his considerable gunbelt and shook his head. 'You ain't drinking now, Slade. You know the rules. Now get back to your post. I'll look after Diamond Jim here since the boss ain't coming back this evening.'

Slade was about to protest, then seeing the assertive posturing of the two men behind the big man he clearly thought better of it. He grinned as a roar went up from the gathering around the pit and the coyote let out a howl of triumph as it stood over the exhausted and savaged body of the vanquished dog. 'We should have come back earlier, Diamond Jim,' he said. 'You could have made me money.'

When Slade had taken his leave, the big man held out a spade-like hand to Wes. 'I'm Burt Kennedy, the ramrod of this outfit.' He touched his eye patch and added, without the trace of a smile, 'The boys call me Hawkeye, on account of the fact that nothing much escapes my good eye.' He signalled to a malevolent looking man with a scar running across the corner of his mouth who was standing behind the bar, gathering a fistful of money from the punters who had bet unwisely on the dog. 'Hey, Gonzalez, bring a bottle and two glasses to the office,' he barked. As he indicated the way towards a door at the other end of the room, Wes noted that the hands of the two heavies were never far from their guns.

Wes accepted the seat on one side of the desk and sat back, his fingertips together, while Hawkeye poured them each a good shot of whiskey. After they had downed their drinks, responding to the ramrod's invitation, he gave an outline of his history; of how he, Diamond Jim, had gained notoriety as a gambler, a drinker and a shootist of some renown. He adopted a modest attitude as he told him about the seven men he had killed, of how he had worked his way around the cow towns of the Panhandle and ended up riding with the Dawsons in Texas.

'But you know how things are,' he said. 'It comes time to move on, see fresh areas of this great country.'

'Texas got too hot, you mean,' Hawkeye suggested with a laugh.

Wes offered a cheroot and, as he struck a light for them both, he smiled. 'You might say that. And as I headed into this territory, I heard about this outfit. You seem to have it pretty well organized around here.'

Hawkeye had been rifling through a batch of papers, which Wes recognized as handbills, mostly printed on Phin Bradley's press, he reckoned. From the middle, he selected the one belonging to his namesake. Wes willed himself to look as nonchalant as possible as the big man scrutinized first the bill, then Wes's face. Finally, the outlaw laid the poster on top of the pile on the table and nodded. 'One thousand dollars!' Hawkeye said, clicking his tongue in admiration. 'Someone thinks you're valuable.' He puffed on his cheroot and leaned on the desk. 'The boss won't be back tonight, maybe not for a few days. He does that, see. But I can say whether you stay or not. We need men who can turn their hands to different aspects of our – business. I'd need to know that Diamond Jim Crane ain't at all squeamish.'

Wes let smoke drift from his lips. 'I guess I can be valuable to you. I've done most things in my time. And I don't scare easy.'

The big ramrod nodded. 'That's good, because we're all living outside the law. All of us need to make enough to one day get back on the right side. And that needs money, big money. Our boss is a good provider that way.'

Wes looked out of the window. The sun was going down and lights had been lit up at the big house. Behind the shutters he fancied that he saw a couple of shadowy figures pacing around an upstairs room. He fancied he knew who they were, and immediately his heart began racing. But he had a part to play, and he had to play it convincingly. An evil leer spread across his face. 'Like I said, Hawkeye, I've done just about most things in my life – and I mean *most* things!'

Hawkeye gave a rough throaty laugh. He held his hand out across the desk. 'I think maybe we could find a spot for you here, Diamond.' He laughed again. 'I guess we're all what you'd call rough diamonds in Rough Valley.'

SIX

After a near sleepless night in a room shared with Wheeler and Slade, Wes awoke at sun-up. He made use of the primitive wash facilities that the bunkhouse had to offer, then followed his nose to the chuck cabin, where 'Chuck' McPhee, the Rough Riders' Scottish cook, a well-fleshed, cheerful fellow with cropped hair and rosy cheeks was labouring happily over skillets and various bubbling pans.

Only one man, Hawkeye, had beaten Wes to breakfast. And he was eating heartily and joshing with McPhee.

'Another healthy man wi' a healthy appetite, I see,' said McPhee, stirring a pan with a long-handled metal spoon. 'Sit and eat. You can have bacon, eggs, beans, steak, sourdough biscuits, or my ain special dish, porridge topped with cream and' – he winked – 'a drop o' Chuck McPhee's special elixir from the old country. Good whisky from the grain, not this tonsil paint stuff they make from rye.'

Wes laughed heartily, but declined both the porridge and McFee's 'elixir,' opting instead for a small steak, a couple of sourdough biscuits and a mug of Arbuckle's.

Hawkeye pointed his fork at the seat opposite him and took a slurp of coffee. 'Hope you slept well, Diamond. I felt kinda guilty about putting you in with Slade and Wheeler.' He grinned and added, 'Mainly 'cos Wheeler is well knowed for having his own portable livestock, and Slade ain't a man who takes too kindly to having his hard-earned coin taken of'n him by some gambling man he's just met.'

Men started shuffling into the chuck cabin with much banter and good-natured cussing at McPhee, who gave as good as he got. Moments later, there was much clambering over benches and back-slapping and leg-pulling, a lot of it directed in Wes's direction.

'The boys may not have liked your poker play-ing, Diamond,' Hawkeye said, 'but they sure enough enjoyed your card juggling.'

'I'll say we did,' came Ned Slade's voice, as he took a seat beside Wes and set his breakfast plate down on the plain table. 'But if'n you'd showed us it afore we started playing cards I'm guessing you woulda ended up playing solitaire.'

Wes joined in the ribbing camaraderie, as he

imagined the real Diamond Jim would have done. And indeed, he had to admit that he'd been rather pleased with the way the evening had gone, in terms of gaining him acceptance among this group of outlaws. Back in his days as a lawman he'd picked up a lot of tips about gambling and card-sharping from long evenings playing cards through cell bars with various clients he'd locked up and been forced to look after until their trials or their sentences had been served out. The honest poker skill he'd learned he put to good use to take a neat pile from those who had chanced their wits against him, while the less than honest sleight-of-hand tricks he had demonstrated afterwards, to emphasize how easy it is to move cards around a deck and keep control of them.

'You're a brave man to show some of these guys those tricks,' said Hawkeye. 'Some of these guys have a reputation for shooting first and asking questions later.'

Wheeler had shuffled over to join them a few moments later, clutching a coffee in one hand and a quirly, the other half of his breakfast, in the other. 'Yeah, but I'm betting they'd be kinda dumb to try that on this *hombre*. I swear he just thought one of those guns into his hand yesterday.'

Wes smiled at the teamster. 'No matter what his trade, a man's got to try to be top of it.'

Gonzalez, the Mexican barkeep, was sitting a

little further down the table. He leaned forward and grinned, his scar making his lop-sided grin look distinctly sinister. 'If you're talking about betting, maybe we could arrange a little competition. A lot of these boys are pretty fast themselves,' he explained. 'Maybe Diamond Jim Crane would like to put his money on his guns.'

Wes leaned forward himself, not a trace of humour on his face. 'Maybe you'd better stick to sick acts like pitting unfair dog fights in that pit of yours. My guns ain't no party pieces. A man can get hurt fooling with guns.'

The grin vanished from Gonzalez's face and he looked to be about to say something further, but he was silenced by a glare from Hawkeye's good eye. 'That's enough; there'll be no shooting competition here. You all know what the boss says about fighting or unnecessary gunplay. Anyone starting trouble in the Riders will leave – one way or another!' He stood and glared at the assembly that had suddenly gone quiet. 'Everyone agree?'

As a chorus of assent ran round the room Hawkeye signalled for McPhee to clear up. Then he walked to the door of the cabin and turned to face them all. 'OK, the day is moving on, let's get to work. I'll be in the boss's office ready to give you your jobs for today. Give me five minutes, then start coming over in threes.'

His eye fell on Wes. 'Diamond, Wheeler and Slade, you come first. I've got a special job for you.'

*

The office of the Rough Riders' boss was on the ground floor of the main house. Like the house itself, it was a far grander place than one would have imagined it to be. The house was of fairly simple construction, yet had decent furnishings and odd attempts at tasteful decoration. It was certainly more sumptuous than one would have expected in an outlaw camp, almost as if the owner had aspirations of respectability.

Wes looked round the office with its maps, ledgers and rolled-up plans and nodded his head appreciatively. 'Anyone would think this was a respectable ranch buried away in the Pintos.' He pointed to the large book that Hawkeye had open in front of him on the desk. 'And you're more organized than a bank here. How come you ain't scared of some darned lawmen coming in after you?'

'Like I told you before,' said Hawkeye, sitting behind the large desk and helping himself to a cigar from a box in front of him. 'This place is damned nigh impregnable and just about impossible to find. Even if they send in an army they'd never find us. And even if they did,' he said slowly as he puffed the cigar into life, 'I figure we could pick them off in one of those box canyons you saw as you came up here.'

'Has anyone ever sent the army in after you?' Wes asked.

'Never,' replied Hawkeye, pushing the cigar box across the desk towards Wes.

'Not until—' began Wheeler, nervously, but a rapid glare from Hawkeye cut him short, much to Slade's amusement. The reaction was all that Wes needed to know. He decided not to pry any more, merely nodded as he struck a light to his cigar.

And indeed, had he required any further confirmation that the two women were being held nearby, he had it as he looked out the window. Chuck McPhee was climbing the steps to the house bearing a tray on which he had set out breakfast for two people.

'OK, Diamond,' went on Hawkeye, leaning over the ledger. 'Here's where you start earning your keep. As you said, this is a business. A tight business and everyone pulls his weight. The boss goes to a lot of trouble creating wealth for us. There's just one thing he won't tolerate. Tell him, Slade.'

Ned Slade grinned malevolently. 'Failure!' he replied simply, emphasizing the word by placing a finger to his temple.

'Bang, bang,' said Wheeler with a humourless grin.

After receiving their orders, the trio left Rough Valley by another route that took them a long circuitous way through the Pintos. On the way they had to run the gauntlet of two lookouts whom Wes recognized as the two heavies who had escorted him into Hawkeye's room the previous evening. Although there were pleasantries passed between them it was obvious to Wes that Slade in particular held no great feelings for either of them.

'Brainless muscle!' the younger man sneered, once they were out of earshot of the last lookout. 'Some day, someone's going to show them—' An evil laugh delivered the meaning of his unfinished sentence.

Eventually, they left the foothills and started picking a path parallel to the main trail towards Hacksville, yet keeping sufficiently far off to remain unseen by anyone riding along the trail. For the most part, Wes and Slade had been in conversation, with only sporadic chipping in from Wheeler. Slade took obvious delight in hearing about Wes's embellished and mainly fictional exploits in the various cow towns along the Panhandle, especially if there were any suggestion of violence or gunplay. From his demeanour, interest and the coldness in his eyes, Wes marked him out as a product of the lawlessness in the Southwest that he so deplored. He looked every inch the sort of young tyro who would draw leather against anyone with a reputation, or a crown to be taken. He also suspected that he might not be too concerned whether his opponent was armed or facing toward him.

'So what about this mysterious boss of yours?' Wes said at last, when a reasonable lapse in the conversation allowed him to change the subject. 'Who is he, and why is he gone so much?'

Slade grinned. 'He's just called the boss. And he's away half the time scouting out jobs and easy pickings for us.'

'And he's the toughest son of a bitch you'll ever meet,' Wheeler added. 'He's so cold-blooded he'd make a rattler seem like a fire-breathing demon. I've seen him—'

'Wheeler's been on the end of his temper a time or two,' Slade cut in with a thin laugh. 'Mind you, Wheeler has a knack of riling folk.'

The teamster shot an angered look at the younger man, took a chew of tobacco and shrugged his shoulders in dismissal.

'Is Hawkeye scared of him?'

'You bet. And that jasper ain't no coward. But he respects him too, account of him having the brains.'

They left the path they had been tracing, crossed the main trail and headed across country, where grass grew in plenty. After a couple of miles they crossed the boundary marker of a ranch, the Jagged J. Immediately, Wes had a mental picture of the portly rancher, Ben Taverner. This was his spread.

'And just what did you mean this morning, Wheeler, when you said there had never been a cause to send in the army after you boys – "until now!" '

Wheeler cast a look at Slade, then spat out a trail of tobacco juice at a mesquite bush. 'I dunno that's any of your business, Diamond. What you think, Slade?'

The younger man grinned. 'Diamond is one of us now, Wheeler.' He had been constructing a quirly as they rode. He struck a light and blew smoke. 'We've sorta kidnapped a couple of women from our last job.' He laughed malevolently. 'Good lookers, the pair of them – know what I mean!' he said suggestively.

Wes forced a lascivious leer to his lips and play-fully punched the youngster on the arm, when in fact he had a great urge to grab the kid by the throat and squeeze the life from him.

They had crossed fields of meandering steers and waded across small riverlets of crystal clear water, then stared to climb a mesa. Once atop they found themselves looking down at the Jagged J ranch. It was certainly in keeping with Ben Taverner's ego. The main house was a two-storeyed, multi-chimneyed place complete with picket fences, flowerbeds and stone-paved and covered verandas. There were two barns, a large bunkhouse and several outbuildings. Strangely, apart from a couple of horses circling in a corral, a thin stream of smoke issuing from a chimney was the only sign of life they could see.

'The boss said it would be like this,' said Slade with a throaty snigger. 'The owner and his whole outfit are holed up in the town, protecting the bank and the fine folk of Hacksville.'

'All of them except a cook with a game leg,' added Wheeler. 'And since old man Taverner don't keep his money at the Hacksville Bank, we happen to know that he keeps it all hid in a strong-box under his study floor.'

Wes nodded and laughed in character. 'Then I guess we just go and get it, huh? But what did Hawkeye say about the cook?'

Slade grinned and looked at Wes with mock indignation. 'Why we treat him gently, of course.'

Ten minutes later, having circled down from the mesa the trio hobbled their horses in a small copse behind the ranch house, then sneaked up to the back door. It was open and through it they heard a man whistling as he rattled some pots and pans in what they assumed was the ranch house kitchen. Without making a noise they unholstered their weapons and silently crept up the back steps.

A half-empty bottle of whiskey upon the table was the first thing they saw, followed by the sight of a middle-aged man swaying as he stood over a water basin scrubbing pots. A coffee pot bubbled away on a stove. The man hiccuped, then made for the stove, only to gasp in bleary-eyed alarm as he caught sight of Wheeler with a peacemaker pointed at him. Whether from genuine courage or booze-induced foolishness, he made a lunge for a large knife that lay on a chopping board beside the basin. But he never reached it, for Slade bounded across the room and viciously pistol-whipped him on the back of the head.

'And that's what I meant when I said treat him gently,' he said with a grin, as he saw Wes scowl at him. 'What's the matter, Diamond? We didn't kill him, did we?'

Wes forced a smile to his lips. 'Why don't I truss him up then, while you two go get the strongbox?'

As the two men left the room, Wes found rope in a cupboard and tied his man up, humanely so as not to cut his wrists, yet firmly so that he would not escape without help, which he hoped would not be too long in coming. But just in case, he left a jug of water nearby so that at least the cook would get water when he regained consciousness.

There was the sound of running feet from another room, a couple of curses, then a woman's scream, followed by a cry of pain from Wheeler.

'Bitch!' he cried. Then there was a thump, like a body falling on the floor.

Wes ran from the kitchen, a Navy Colt appearing in his hand as he did so. He half skidded as he entered a room that was undoubtedly the rancher's study. But what alarmed him was the sight of Wheeler standing nursing a bite in his hand, while Slade stood grinning over the body of a woman, lying face down on the floor.

'Well lookie here, Diamond,' said Slade. 'A bonus

for us.' His eyes gleamed lecherously as he took in the curves and long raven hair that had tumbled about her shoulders. 'I guess we could have some fun before we go. What d'you say, Wheeler?'

He reached down and pulled the woman up, just as she started to recover. She shook her head groggily. 'You . . . you bastards!' she cried. 'Just wait until my fiancé gets back. He'll take—'

She had raised her head defiantly, her eyes taking in Slade, Wheeler and Wes. And in that moment Wes recognized Betsy, just as she saw through his disguise. Her eyes widened in surprise. 'You!' she gasped. 'Why, what the—?'

But Wes gave her no chance to say more. He crossed the room with two strides and knocked her out with a swift right uppercut.

Slade and Wheeler looked utterly shocked. 'God damn it, Diamond, why'd you do that?' Slade demanded.

Wes blew air through his lips. 'You boys should be thanking me for saving you. I recognized that calico queen – with good cause,' he explained, suggestively putting a hand on his groin and grimacing as he shook his head. 'You may think you'd be getting a good time with that whore, but you'd sure as hell pay for it later. By the look of that ring on her finger I'd say she'd finally hood-winked some poor sucker into making an honest woman out of her.'

And without more ado he returned to the

kitchen and brought back some rope. Like the cook he tied her firmly, yet not so well that she wouldn't be able to set herself free in time. But just in case she came round before they had found the strongbox, he gagged her.

Fortunately, the boss's instructions as to where to find the box were dead right and they had left the ranch within five minutes.

It was almost evening by the time they returned to Rough Valley and turned over their loot to Hawkeye. The one-eyed outlaw laughed as Slade recounted their adventure with the calico queen.

'Go get some food, boys,' he said, 'then meet me in the saloon and I'll buy you all a drink.'

The saloon was busy as usual by the time they returned, their stomachs full and their thirst for liquor stoked up. Keen though he was to keep his wits about him, even Wes was looking forward to a slug or two of tonsil paint. Hawkeye was at the bar talking to a group of men. He turned and waved the trio over.

'Got another new man this evening,' he announced to them. 'Another sinner from Texas. Say how-do to Buck Brewster.'

The tall man dressed in black turned at the bar and nodded to the trio of riders. Although he didn't realize it, Wes and he had passed each other on the outskirts of Hacksville.

SEVEN

Ben Taverner looked fit to bust a blood vessel as he stomped up and down the length of the Lucky Belle Saloon. Anxiety, fury and utter frustration all seemed to have crowded into his life and demanded an expression on his normally confident and calm face.

'I'm going to kill that damned judge!' he growled venomously at Red O'Leary, the town sheriff, who stood nervously at the front of a crowd of the local citizens, while the little rancher ranted and raved. 'He could have killed my sweet Betsy. Damned near did kill old Sam, my cook. Just about busted his head open and then trussed him up like a chicken.' His eyes bulged with renewed anger. 'The bastard even trussed Betsy up after he knocked her out.'

'How ... how's she doing, boss?' Sheriff O'Leary asked nervously, unable to refrain from addressing his employer in a deferential manner.

'She's in shock, the doc said. He's got her staying with her friend Laura until I get this all sorted out.'

Red O'Leary's eyes brightened. 'I guess I ought to pay her a visit then, take a statement.'

'You damned well will not!' barked Ben Taverner. 'The doc says she needs rest.' His chest rose pompously. 'He even said I can't see her for a few hours. No, Red, you're gonna concentrate on getting these outlaws once and for all. And that means getting that thieving, murdering judge who's been hoodwinking us all.'

There was a chorus of whiskey-soaked approval. It spurred Taverner's ego and he went on, 'I knew I should have taken charge yesterday. But no, we let ourselves be hoodwinked by—'

'No one hoodwinked anybody, Ben Taverner, you darned fool!'

The rancher spun round to face the entrance, where Phin Bradley and Hiram G. Lanchester had just come in. His already purple face went puce. 'Don't you call me names Mister high-and-mighty Newspaperman! And you know damned well that judge feller, whatever he calls himself, fooled us all. Why, he's been one of those outlaws all along. I guess he's been feeding them information. My Betsy saw him with her own eyes, as he and two others robbed my very own ranch,' and, as if he could hardly credit his own words, his face showed total bewilderment for a few moments. 'Then he

92

punched her straight in the face. A woman! He hit a woman for Chris'sakes.'

And an angry chorus rang round the room, with jeers of contempt for anyone low enough to do violence to a woman – especially the fiancée of Ben Taverner, the richest man in the area.

Hiram was leaning heavily on a crutch. He held up his free hand and slowly the crowd quietened. 'Mr Taverner, I don't doubt that your fiancée was struck somehow by Wes Talbot, but I can assure you it could only have been done because he had no choice.'

There were shouts of disapproval. Ben Taverner shook his head angrily. 'I say he's a lying skunk and a crook.'

Phin Bradley took an angry step towards him, ignoring Red O'Leary who shoved himself forward as he perceived there might be a threat to his boss. 'I said you were a fool, Taverner, and I meant it. Wes Talbot is the best judge we've ever had around here. He's as honest as the day is long. He certainly wouldn't hurt a woman unless he had no choice.'

The portly rancher sneered. 'And just how come he was with these desperadoes anyhow? Didn't you hear me? They were robbing my ranch. They've stolen a strongbox with—' He shook his head, deciding rapidly that no one needed to know how much he had been taken for. 'How come a judge would be robbing my ranch?'

Another voice entered the discussion as Dexter

Bolton came in, letting the batwing doors swing behind him. 'Because he's there under cover. He figured that the only way to get my Evie and Pam back would be by infiltrating the Rough Riders. Clearly he has done just what he set out to do.'

'Or he's joined them for real!' replied Ben Taverner. 'I thought he was going to contact the military?'

'He did that before he disguised himself and left,' said Hiram.

Red O'Leary, who had taken virtually no part shook his head. 'I checked this afternoon. He didn't send any message. The army knew nothing about the robbery or the kidnappings.'

It was the turn of Phin, Hiram and Dexter Bolton to look startled. Before they could say anything, Ben Taverner went on, 'Like I just said, I should have taken charge yesterday, before we lost a day. Like it or not, Bradley,' he said, jabbing the air in Phin's direction, 'I'm going to get your daughter back.' He turned to the banker. 'And your wife, Bolton.'

Phin began to protest, but Sheriff O'Leary put a firm hand on his shoulder. 'Any more trouble, Bradley, and I'm going to arrest you for obstruction. Take my advice and listen to the boss.'

Taverner nodded and thumped the bar with a fist. 'Tactics! That's what we need. Tomorrow morning me, Red and some of the boys are gonna go in, capture one of that gang and – persuade him to take us into their hide-out. Only this time we'll have all the firepower we need.'

Dexter Bolton chewed his lip, then nodded his head, as if having made a serious decision. 'I'm sorry, men,' he said to Phin and Hiram, 'but I guess that Mr Taverner could have a point. Who's to say that he hasn't joined the Rough Riders and helped them kidnap Evie and Pam?'

Phin looked at the banker incredulously. 'I think this has turned your mind, Dexter. You can't be serious? A big posse going in there could spell out a death sentence for the girls.'

Dexter shook his head, like a man no longer certain of anything, like a man who had lost his bank's money and his wife all in one go. But with the uncertainty there was also a look of determination. 'I'm going with them to get my Evie back.'

As Phin and Hiram left to a background mumble interspersed with the odd jibe and jeer, Ben Taverner began to outline his master plan for the morrow.

Wes played cards and drank a shot or two from the bottle placed on the poker table by Hawkeye. In the background, he was aware of other men playing cards at a couple of adjoining tables, while the majority caroused noisily at the bar, many berating Gonzalez for failing to provide them with any kind of blood sport to bet on. Despite his calm and at times jocular appearance, Wes's mind was racing anxiously. He was conscious that he had spent a whole day without actually contacting the two women, even though he was pretty sure where they were imprisoned.

His mind was not fully on the game, so that he was down on his pile, much to the glee of some of the players, and the wariness of others who half thought that this was a ploy on the part of the famed gambler, Diamond Jim Crane, to lull them into false security. Yet it was not just anxiety over the girls, he was also deeply conscious of Buck Brewster sitting opposite him, who kept scrutinizing him every few moments. And indeed, Wes had also been scrutinizing his poker-playing opponent – sure that he recognized certain features that reminded him of Daniel Meldrum, whom he had tried and sentenced to death.

'You sure aren't having much luck tonight, pardner,' Buck Brewster said. 'For your sake I hope your luck changes.'

It was an innocent enough remark, yet one which could have had two if not three hidden meanings. Wes made a witty rejoinder, but noted the other possibilities. Was the man being guardedly hostile? Was he somehow warning him? Did he know that Wes was aware that he too was there under a disguised name? All these thoughts ran through his head as he picked up his next hand, yet there was something intangible, something that you could not quite put your finger on. It was a tone, an inflection perhaps. Something in the man's very speech that struck a chord.

As he fanned his cards in front of him, he saw the gimlet eyes staring at him, reaffirming his suspicion that the man sitting opposite him was in fact the brother of Daniel Meldrum: it was the man they called the Deacon.

Slade and Wheeler had both been drinking heavily, Wes had noticed, so it was a relief to him to hear them both snoring noisily, as if each had finally fallen into a drunken stupor when they retired late that night. He lay in the dark for about fifteen minutes, allowing his eyes to accustom themselves to the faint light of a waning moon, then he started to make his move.

He had climbed into his bunk with his clothes on, having merely removed his boots. Now he picked them up in the darkness and tiptoed across the room to the door. Once outside he slipped on his footwear, instinctively checked his weapons and then ran softly through the shadows to the livery barn, where he selected three bridles. He then went to the corral fence and hung them on a post so that he would be able to locate them without too much trouble. The bay was in the corral and it snickered when it sensed his presence.

Just be ready when I come back with the girls, he said silently to himself, as if trying to send his thought messages to the horse. His mission was desperate, he knew, and none too certain of succeeding. It was a gamble, a huge gamble that was going to depend on the fact that the whole outlaw gang had just about drunk itself into insensibility. You and two of your pals here are going to have to take us out of this valley, he thought, looking at the bay and gaining some comfort from the thought that its intelligent head almost looked as though it was looking straight at him with understanding. 'And you're going to have to do it bareback. Won't be time for saddles.'

Then, turning and again moving through the shadows he made his way up to the big house, which was in darkness except for a single upstairs room where he was sure the girls were being kept, and a lamp shining through the window of an adjoining hall or landing.

I guess that's where the guard will be sitting, he thought, as he mounted the steps and found a window that he could slide up. The geography of the place he had registered the day before, and he reckoned that Pam and Evelyn would be fretting in the room directly above.

The sound of a man snoring greeted him as he silently mounted the darkened staircase. On reaching the landing he saw Chuck McPhee sprawled out on an easy chair, with a half-empty bottle of his special elixir on the floor beside him, together with a bunch of tell-tale keys. Moving around the edge of the circle of light from the oil lamp, his hand strayed to the handle of his gun. It would be the matter of a moment to club the Scottish cook and put him out of action for certain. But there was something about the man that he had rather taken to, which stayed his hand. McPhee didn't seem a bad man; he was just the jovial cook of an outlaw band. Besides, he reasoned, a blow to a man's head could knock him out, or just as easily maim or kill him. If he could get away from Rough Valley without shedding blood needlessly, that's what he was going to do.

He retrieved the keys and silently unlocked the door, entering the room with barely a sound. Indeed, neither of the two women sitting on either side of a small candlelit table playing cards noticed him enter and shut the door behind him, until his footstep made a floorboard creak. Then they both turned, anxiety written across their faces as they saw his shadowy form at the door.

'Who?' began Pam.

'No!' shrieked Evelyn. 'Don't—'

But Wes put a finger to his lips and strode across the room into the light. 'Sh, Pam, Evie – it's me, Wes!' And he pulled off his Stetson for them to recognize him, despite his bleached blond hair.

'Wes! My God!' gasped Pam, rising and throwing herself into his arms and hugging him close. 'Thank God, you've come. How many of you—?'

The sound of Evelyn Bolton's chair scraping on wood as she abruptly stood up brought them both to attention, and they turned to look at her as she backed away, eyes wide with horror, her hand covering her mouth, stifling a scream that threatened to bubble to the surface.

'It's OK, Evie,' Pam soothed. 'It's Wes. We're going to get out of here.'

But Evelyn was staring past them and tremulously raising a hand to point behind them.

Wes was about to look when he felt the unmistakable prod of a gun barrel in his back. Simultaneously, he saw Pam gasp, then, 'D . . . don't move, Wes, it . . . it's—'

There was a soft laugh, then a man's voice. 'They call me the Deacon,' he said. 'And I'm guessing that your rightful name ain't Diamond Jim Crane, is it? I'm guessing that you're Talbot – Judge Wes Talbot?'

Wes had raised his hands. He nodded his head. 'I'm Talbot. And I guess you know that I'm here to rescue these two ladies from this band of cutthroats.'

He felt his guns being raised from his belt one at a time, and the shells being ejected on to the floor. Then he heard the guns land with soft thuds on one of the beds on the other side of the room.

'I heard about these two ladies being kidnapped when I visited your town,' Cash Meldrum replied. 'And I heard that you'd taken control of the town, and then gone missing yourself.'

'How did you get here?'

'It's my job, Judge – tracking scum.'

The gun barrel was pressed unwaveringly in his back and Wes knew he was helpless. He had no weapon, except logic and reason. 'I guess you think that you and I have business,' he said.

'Darned right we do!' Cash snapped back. 'You had my little brother hanged – for crimes he didn't do.'

Evelyn Bolton gave a short sob, her eyes panic-stricken. It was clear that the woman was close to hysteria.

'You the Bolton bitch?'

Evelyn backed further away and Pam stepped in front of her friend, as if to shield her. 'Yes that's Evelyn Bolton,' Pam said with spirit. ' And don't you even think of going near her, after what your brother did to her.'

Cash's eyes narrowed. 'My brother didn't do anything to her, and she knows it. And I'm here to get the truth out of her. I'll have justice for my kid brother if'n it's the last thing I do.'

'Listen, Meldrum,' said Wes. 'Let's think of how to get out of here, and then we can—'

But he had no time to finish. The Deacon raised his gun and brought it down savagely on Wes's head. He slumped to the floor, diving into a pool of darkness, oblivious to everything except Cash Meldrum's voice. 'Lying is the language of Satan. Now I'm going to get the truth!'

*

It seemed to Wes that he had been lying for an indeterminate time, although in reality it had been barely more than a few seconds, thanks to an innate thick skull, and a desperation that was driving him to save the woman he loved. He raised his head groggily to see Pam lying on the floor, blood trickling from a cut on her lip. His heart lurched for a second, then when he saw her lift her head he felt an immense relief. Then he heard the sound of a slap, and Cash Meldrum's raised voice.

'Tell the truth, you bitch! Why did you lie about my brother?'

Wes was on his feet in a moment. That Cash Meldrum's mind had gone; that he had been driven mad with hate and the desire for revenge was all too clear. But it was the noise of his raised voice that caused him the most anxiety, for it was sure to bring outlaws down on them. And Evelyn, never an emotionally robust woman was sure to snap. She looked terrified as she tried to back further away from him, to bury herself into the woodwork of the wall.

Wes launched himself across the room and caught Meldrum in a bear-hug. They crashed to the floor, and Wes having the initiative, took the opportunity to knock the bounty hunter's gun from his hand. His fist rose and fell, slamming Meldrum's head against the floor. Yet it was only a temporary edge, for immediately Meldrum shot up and head-butted Wes above the nose. He fell back and immediately Meldrum was on him. Back and forth they rolled on the floor.

Wes vaguely heard Evelyn screaming and Pam trying to calm her down. But all his energies were focused on getting the upper hand against the Deacon.

And then there seemed to be people everywhere. Men laughing, boots kicking both him and his opponent. Then a gunshot rang out and a woman screamed.

EIGHT

Wes and Cash Meldrum were roughly tossed into the fighting pit in the Rough Valley 'saloon'. They had been pulled apart, disarmed and softened up a little, then manhandled out of the big house while the two women were silenced with threats before being locked up under McPhee's care. They pulled themselves up to stand warily a little distance apart, each conscious of the leering ring of faces looking down on them. Already Gonzalez was gabbling away, taking money and bets. From the short time he had been a member of the Rough Riders Wes had realized their love of blood sports, and being himself deposited in the cock-fighting ring, he knew that things looked bad.

'You really are a gambling man, ain't you, Diamond?' laughed Hawkeye, standing above them like a ringmaster in some bizarre circus. 'Did you figure that you could just walk in and steal our two female guests from under our noses?'

Ned Slade was standing leering beside the one-eyed outlaw. Wes noted that he seemed a lot soberer than he had expected him to be. Indeed, they all did. 'I reckon he had other plans for them, Hawkeye,' Slade said suggestively. 'Diamond's a man ruled by his trouser friend. He saved Wheeler and me from getting the clap from that Jagged J whore.'

So they still didn't realize who he was, Wes pondered. And so he forced a rueful smile to his lips. 'Guess that means that you owe me,' he said. 'How's about putting in a word with the boys to get me out of here – for old time's sake.'

Wheeler appeared further along the ring. 'Hell no, Diamond. We couldn't stop the boys' fun could we?' He guffawed, showing broken, yellow-stained teeth. 'Besides, maybe we'll just put some money on you – for old time's sake,' he added mockingly.

Slade grinned. 'Yeah, and if you make it outa that ring, maybe we'll cut you in on our winnings.'

'Then again, maybe not!' cried Wheeler.

Wes smiled up at Hawkeye. 'So what are you boys aiming at? Want us to race round and round this pit?'

Howls of laughter and cries of derision echoed round the great room as the mob began to bray for blood. But Hawkeye silenced them with raised arms. 'Comedian ain't you, Diamond. Well, maybe you will get a chance at a last laugh, but first we wanna know what Brewster was up to.'

Cash Meldrum had been silent all this time. 'I had business with one of them.'

Howls of approval went up, mixed with several lewd and lascivious comments.

'How did you know who they were?' Hawkeye challenged.

'I heard in Hacksville,' the Deacon replied, his face impassive and emotionless. 'And her and me will have business later.'

'Later?' cried Hawkeye, sardonically. 'Mister, there might not be any later for you.' Then, addressing them both, 'We ain't exactly got law here,' he said to more hoots of derision and merriment. 'But we got a kinda code. And that is that no one steals from the gang, or goes against the common good. That means no card-cheating, no gunplay and no stealing of assets.'

'Especially not female assets!' Slade piped in, to general ribald hilarity.

Wes shook his head innocently. 'We weren't stealing properly,' he protested cheerfully. 'Leastways, I was just planning to steal a look.' He glanced at Cash Meldrum. 'This feller was the one who had business.'

This time even Hawkeye laughed. 'So you were protecting our interests.'

'That's right,' Wes continued, keeping up his part as the devil-may-care gambler, Diamond Jack Crane. 'I was looking after the gang's assets.'

Gonzalez prodded Hawkeye. 'You gonna tell them the rules, Hawkeye?'

Again the big man roared with laughter. 'The boys are getting impatient,' he said with an evil leer on his face. 'I guess you two have the idea by now. This here's a continuation of the fight you started up at the big house. Last man standing wins. And the rules—' He turned and spat into the ring. 'There are no rules!'

Pam had a time of trying to calm Evelyn down. It had been a cruel blow to be given a hope of rescue, only to have it dashed away. And even though she felt for her friend having been through a rape, having witnessed a massacre, then been kidnapped by a band of outlaws, still she was more worried for Wes. Indeed, her heart ached more than she thought it possible. The man she loved, who had asked her to marry him, had come to rescue her; only to get caught and carried off to goodness only knew what purpose. At least she had not heard any gunfire, which suggested that there had been no summary execution.

Just how had that man, the Deacon, managed to get into the Rough Riders, camp? She had heard the big man they called Hawkeye address Wes as Diamond, so clearly Wes's disguise had been successful. Would the Deacon keep quiet, or would he reveal that Wes was a judge, a hated figure among the outlaw breed?

'Pam, what – what are they going to do with Wes and that – that murderer?' Evelyn Bolton asked, chewing her lip anxiously. 'What will they do with . . . us?'

'Hush, Evie,' Pam soothed. 'Wes will have made some contingency plans, I bet. You'll be seeing Dexter before too long, believe me.' Yet despite her comforting words, she herself wondered whether they'd ever see anyone they knew again.

If the worst came to the worst, she wondered if she would have the courage to do what she would have to do.

Wes's mind was racing. So the whole thing had been a set-up! The whole gang drinking to seeming insensibility; Chuck McPhee's apparent drunken stupor and the ease with which he had made it unchallenged to the big house. He had fallen straight into the trap, as had Cash Meldrum.

They had both immediately dropped into fighting postures and started stalking one another round the cockpit, to accompanying jeers and whistles of encouragement from the mob above.

Cash Meldrum was taller than Wes by a couple of inches and probably had a weight advantage of about six or seven pounds. He didn't look as if he had a spare ounce of fat on him. And he moved like a cougar, like a natural hunter.

'Well, Mister *Diamond*,' he hissed, his face showing more emotion than it had when he was facing

Hawkeye and the mob a few moments before, 'I'm going to enjoy this. Think of it as justice.'

Wes felt his anger suddenly flare. He knew that Cash Meldrum was again referring to the hanging of his brother, as if his brother had been an innocent man. But Wes had sentenced the younger Meldrum to death after reviewing utterly damning evidence of his guilt, and after hearing the testimony of Evelyn Bolton, a woman Wes knew quite well, and who also happened to be his fiancée's best friend. Her brutal rape had traumatized her to the point of near complete nervous breakdown. A look at the face now contorted with hate made Wes realize that the man had clearly gone mad with grief over his brother, so that revenge was now his sole motivation. Yet it was misguided, because his brother was a worthless rapist and murderer who clearly had deserved the rope.

And with that thought in his mind Wes moved in as fast as a rattlesnake and landed two swift jabs that rattled Meldrum's jaw and caused him to stagger back.

'That's a little justice from me,' said Wes, a faint smile hovering over his lips. 'Call it payback for that blow on the back of my head.' And to add a barb to the jabs, he added, 'Only a cowardly cur hits from behind.'

In reply, Meldrum moved in with his arms flailing. Wes parried a couple successfully, and then caught one on the temple, instantly appreciating the power of his opponent. 'How d'you like them from the front then!' said Meldrum, through gritted teeth.

Wes shook his head. 'I've felt harder,' he said, ducking a swinging hook and countering with a barrage of body blows delivered with punishing effect.

But the fight went both ways. Within moments both men had bruises developing and cuts on their faces and fists. And all the time Gonzalez was taking bet and counter-bet from the bloodthirsty mob above.

'Ten on diamond!'

'Twenty says Buck Brewster will break Diamond's neck.'

None of the comments were consciously taken in by the two fighters. All they were aware of were the shouts, screams and cacophony of cussing. To the crowd they were no better than the cocks, dogs and snakes that they bet on each day. No one would mourn their deaths, other than for the loss of their betting money.

Wes's muscles ached and his breathing was coming hard. Yet he felt pleased to see that the Deacon was in no better state. So far it had been pretty evenly matched. Only stamina would sort them out.

Then suddenly, as Wes stepped backwards, dodging a real haymaker from Meldrum, his foot slipped and he felt himself fighting for balance. In that flickering moment, Meldrum saw the opening and threw himself on Wes, his arms encircling his chest and crushing him in a bear hug, their joint momentum hurling them on to the floor of the cockpit.

Wes gasped as he felt an excruciating pain in his chest, as something seemed to snap. He divined correctly that a rib had just broken. Yet the bounty hunter's grip did not lessen a jot.

'I'm going to break them all!' Meldrum hissed, making it clear in spades to Wes that his opponent was only too aware of the damage he had inflicted, and that he was about to press home his advantage maliciously.

The crowd seemed to sense blood and were urging the fighters on.

Bad though the pain was, worse was the fact that Wes was unable to move his arms or his chest, so that he slowly began to suffocate. He felt consciousness start to ebb away.

'You're – gonna – die – now!' Cash Meldrum grated.

And those words gave Wes the sudden strength to fight back. A voice inside his mind told him that if he let Cash Meldrum finish him off then the two women would be as good as dead. He forced his head forward and sank his teeth into the Deacon's ear, slicing through the cartilage and tearing the lobe off with a yank of his head. Meldrum howled in agony and let go, one hand going to his ear while the other drove down towards Wes's face.

But it was merely a glancing blow for Wes had turned, spat out the flesh and blood and was painfully gasping air into his injured chest. Death was no longer imminent, but if he was to survive he knew that he would have to finish his opponent quickly. He lashed out with his knee, catching the bigger man in the groin, causing him to jack-knife in pain. And as he did so, Wes rolled over and struggled to his feet, in time to meet the Deacon as he too forced himself to stand.

Cash Meldrum swung with all his might, but Wes ducked, rose and delivered an uppercut that almost lifted the Deacon off his feet. He landed on his back, his arms splayed out, totally unconscious.

Wes stood gasping for air clutching his injured chest with both hands. Up above, the Rough Riders' mob was going crazy. Wes looked up and saw Wheeler and Slade grinning down at him, both of them giving a thumbs up sign.

'Did you make money on me, boys?' he gasped, forcing a lop-sided grin.

He didn't hear Hawkeye land in the pit behind him until it was too late. For the second time that night he felt a gun butt smack into the back of his head, then he felt himself pitch across the body of Cash Meldrum, before he too lost consciousness.

Daybreak saw Sheriff Red O'Leary send his posse into the Pintos, via the Hanging Rock entrance.

The men were all heavily armed and went in single file. The sheriff was, of course, only nominally in charge, for Ben Taverner had already instructed them on how they were going to outwit the outlaws.

'They're bound to have one, maybe two look-outs here at the most,' he had explained. 'We'll go in while it's still half night so visibility will be poor. We send in two front-riders and give them enough space so as they'll think there are just the two of them to deal with.' His piggy eyes had twinkled. 'Then, when they're challenged, we ride in fast and get 'em.'

Red had thought the plan sounded naïve, but Taverner paid his wages and had been good to him over all the years he had worked for him. Apart from that his own venture into the Pintos after the Rough Riders had been less than successful, so he readily endorsed the plan.

Tom Chambers and Roddie Pool, two young, devil-may-care punchers, had volunteered to be the lead men. They ambled along the ill-lit trail and, after about a hundred yards, found themselves under fire. Or at least, they felt the wind of a bullet zinging over their heads and immediately rode into the shadows of the rocky walls. As soon as they had made themselves invisible in the darkness, they drew their guns and sent a hail of bullets in the direction of the shot. And with that fusillade echoing around the rocks Red, Ben and the rest of the posse, about a dozen men, came thundering along the pass, guns drawn and blazing to create the impression that a small army was on the move.

Another single shot rang out, biting dust from the middle of the trail between Tom and Roddie. It was immediately followed by the sound of a horse starting into a gallop further ahead.

'There he goes!' cried Tom, jubilantly. 'One man on a roan.'

And off they went, the whole posse strung out in a line. The trail opened up after careering round a number of tight corners.

'We're gaining on him, boss,' Roddie Pool yelled over his shoulder, at the same time loosing off a couple of shots from his Colt .45 at the retreating figure.

The trail opened to allow several horses to ride along swiftly at once, and they saw the fleeing outlaw's horse make its way into the first of three canyon entrances.

'Fifty bucks to the man that brings down that horse!' cried Ben Taverner.

'But shoot low,' bellowed Red O'Leary, 'we need that man alive.'

Into the canyon they chased him, and saw him making for a narrow channel between two massive boulders. A hundred yards ahead of them he passed through the gap then turned and fired a handgun.

Almost immediately there was a thunderous

explosion above the two boulders and a huge cloud of flame, smoke and rock erupted, obscuring the gap through which the outlaw had gone. The posse reined up and watched the cloud slowly settle, only to reveal that the gap was now sealed with a fall of rock.

'The bastards!' cried Ben. 'They've shut us out.'

No sooner were his words out than there was another explosion from behind them. All fourteen men turned round and saw another cloud of flame and smoke mushrooming upwards.

'My God!' breathed Dexter Bolton. 'They haven't shut us out – they've shut us in!'

As the men of the Hacksville posse realized that they had fallen into a trap, the bullets started to hail down on them.

NINE

The far-off noise of two explosions impinged vaguely upon Wes's mind, raising him from utter insensibility to a nauseating swirl of groggy consciousness and pain. The nausea came first, a powerful eruption that forced him to retch until his stomach was pumped dry. Then came the pain; all at once his head felt as if someone had tried to open it at the back with a cleaver; his chest burned with every difficult breath and his left eye would barely open. Worst of all was the realization that he could not move his hands to touch any of those painful parts, for he was sitting on a dirt floor propped against a wall with his hands bound behind his back and his feet tied at the ankles.

'So you ain't dead after all,' came a sardonic voice from somewhere off to his right. In the dim light of the cellar, for this he perceived it to be, he made out the equally battered and bound Cash Meldrum.

'Figured I'd killed you after all,' Meldrum added.

Wes spat to try to remove the acrid taste of vomit from his mouth. 'You wouldn't have known anything, Meldrum. I knocked you out fair and square. Someone knocked me out from behind after I'd finished you off.'

'You call chewing my ear off fair and square?' the Deacon asked sarcastically. 'But it don't matter none, just delays the outcome a while longer.'

'Meaning?'

'Meaning I'm going to kill you anyway – Mister high-and-mighty Judge Talbot!'

Wes ignored the use of his name, just as Meldrum had ignored the use of his. Instead he asked, 'What you reckon those explosions were?'

Neither of them heard the cellar door open.

'That's a little surprise for your friends,' came a sneering voice that Wes recognized as belonging to Ned Slade. He was carrying a box and as he came across the cellar he dropped to one knee in front of Wes. 'Let's have a look-see at that chest, Diamond. Reckon by the sound of that snap last night that you busted a rib.'

Wes forced a grin. 'That's what I figured too.'

'Well, lemme see if'n I can't make it more comfortable,' said Slade. And so saying he opened Wes's shirt, examined his rib cage and identified the area where the rib sprung with telltale painfulness. From the box he took a large bandage and circled it several times round Wes's chest. 'It'll hurt some for a few days, but at least that'll let you breathe without thinking you've been stabbed each time.'

'I'm obliged, Ned,' Wes said, grateful despite his inner loathing for the outlaw.

Slade grinned back. 'No sweat. What're friends for, Diamond?' he said with an ingratiating tone that somehow failed to ring true. 'Besides, the boss said I gotta patch you up as best I can, then we can all have a little get-together.'

He drew a knife out of his belt and stood up in front of Cash Meldrum.

'You gonna help your friend get rid of his opponent now?' Meldrum asked sneeringly.

Slade ran a finger along the blade, wincing for a moment as a trickle of blood appeared on his finger. He sucked his finger then grinned maliciously. 'It's a sharp knife this. Just like a surgeon's scalpel. How would you like me to trim the jagged edges of'n that ear wound?'

The Deacon shrugged his shoulders. 'Do anything you want – if you want me to add you to my death list, kid.'

Slade laughed, his eyes registering little emotion, Wes noticed. Once again there was about the young man a look of madness, as if he was happy leading a violent life and someday expected to die a violent death. He hefted the knife for a moment then shook his head dismissively.

'Wheeler!' he yelled. 'Hey, Wheeler, get your ass down here and gimme a hand.'

Then he kneeled down and with a single sweep sliced through the ropes that bound the Deacon's ankles. 'On your feet, tough guy. We're all gonna go see the boss man.

Pam and Evelyn had spent a miserable night during which neither had slept a wink. Evelyn had seemed to sink into a pit of despair and had spent hours whimpering and moaning for Dexter. Pam had spent the night trying to work out some sort of plan to escape. Yet for all her wit and all her inventiveness, no matter how ingeniously she thought she could get McPhee, their jailor, into a position whereby she could attack him, she always came back to the inescapable fact that even if she could overpower him, they could never get past all of the outlaws in the Rough Riders' camp.

Yet something had happened overnight. She had been all too aware that the outlaws had done something to Cash Meldrum and her beloved Wes, at least witnessed by all the noise they'd heard for a while after they'd taken them away. She assumed that they had been beaten up, since she refused to allow herself to even contemplate that they could have been tortured – or worse.

But then sometime around four o'clock, she estimated, there had been a flurry of activity outside, followed by what seemed to be a mass movement of horses.

'Another raid somewhere,' she said to herself. And if she was right in her conjecture it would mean that the main mass of the gang would be away for some hours. Their best, indeed possibly their only chance of escape, would have to be taken soon. But how? With what to help? After Wes and Meldrum had been taken away, McPhee had removed everything that could possibly be used as a weapon. But maybe, just maybe, she thought—

'Pam!' Evelyn whispered urgently. 'Do you – do you think I'll ever see Dexter again?'

Pam put a comforting arm about her friend's shoulders. 'Of course you will, Evie. Of course you will.'

At that very moment Dexter Bolton wished that he could have turned back the clock a few days. So that he could be back in his own bank, waiting for Evie to bring him his lunch. In fact, at that moment, as he lay behind the carcass of a horse with a bullet in his shoulder, he pretty much wished that he could be anywhere else.

By his own admission Dexter Bolton was not a brave man. He was not even a particularly clever man. An aptitude for mathematics and a love of numbers had catapulted him into banking, which had been regarded as one of the safest of professions. At least that is what he had believed before he had moved to the Southwest.

When he had first met Evelyn two years before, when she moved to Hacksville to take up a book-keeping job, Dexter had thought her the most beautiful woman he'd ever seen. And she was a beautiful woman. He had been happy when she accepted his offer of a position at his bank, even happier that time that she agreed to have dinner with him, and absolutely ecstatic when, three months later, she agreed to be his wife.

Then had come the stagecoach massacre, her rape and the breakdown. They'd gotten through that, thanks in no small measure to Pam Bradley, only for the Rough Riders to rob the bank and kidnap her. No, Dexter chided himself, he had no right to feel sorry for himself, he was here as a member of the Hacksville posse to rescue her and that was what he was going to do. If he survived, that was.

'Damn it!' he cursed, as another bullet hammered into the carcass of his horse. He chanced a look over its chest at the four remaining riders who continued to charge up and down the length of the box canyon vainly trying to get a bead on the men on the rim rock above who were picking them off like flies. Dexter felt a surge of anger and despair. Anger at the way they'd let themselves be trapped so easily, and despair that it was unlikely he'd ever see Evie again.

So far it had been a slaughter. Fourteen men had ridden into the canyon that the outlaws had sealed off with dynamite. Four had died in the opening salvo from the Rough Riders. Four more, including Dexter, were wounded and sheltering as best they could behind their slain mounts. Two more, Ben Taverner and Roddie Pool, were pinned down behind rocks, while Red O'Leary, Tom Chambers and two other Jagged J men charged back and forth, sitting ducks who seemed intent on trying to keep the horses moving in the hope that somehow they'd catch sight of a way out of the canyon, or at least keep the horses, their best hope of escape, alive for as long as possible.

'Keep moving, boys,' yelled Ben Taverner. 'Draw their fire and me and Roddie will pick them off.'

Dexter cursed the pompous rancher, who had so far not even come close to hitting one of the outlaws. And still, having led them into a death trap he seemed oblivious to his personal inadequacies as a tactician and a leader, and was even now giving orders that could only make matters worse.

The four riders had scattered and were riding separately, either riding as low in the saddle as they could, or riding supported by one stirrup as they hid along one flank, Indian style, to make themselves as hard to hit as possible. But it was a well nigh impossible task, for the horses were visibly tiring, and the riders were exhausted in their attempts to dodge lead.

Ten yards from Dexter, the top of Tom Chambers's head exploded in a mass of blood and brain pulp. Dexter watched aghast as the horse galloped onwards, Tom's body staying upright in the saddle for a few moments before falling back and somersaulting into the dust. Only a bare twenty yards further on, the horse crashed to the ground as a barrage of bullets hammered into its brain.

There was the sound of much laughter and cries of glee from the bloodthirsty bunch atop the rim rock.

Ben Taverner stood and let off a couple of shots. 'Blast you bastards to hell!' he screeched, ducking back down as an answering hail of bullets sent him scuttling for cover. Then, 'Keep going boys,' he urged the three remaining riders. 'I'll think of something to get us out of here.'

McPhee herded the two women at gunpoint down the stairs.

'You don't look the type who would shoot women,' Pam said, searchingly.

The Scotsman chuckled. 'Lassie, they say ye shouldna judge a book by its cover. Do you really think I'd be cooking for the Rough Riders if'n I could help it? Maybe I'm a rougher, more desperate man than you'd think.' He chuckled again, an evil edge appearing in his laugh. 'I wouldn't risk it if I was you.'

'Don't – don't shoot us,' whimpered Evelyn Bolton. 'We'll go wherever you want. Just don't hurt us.'

They were ushered into the large study they had seen earlier, when Hawkeye, the evil-looking one-eyed outlaw had told them that as long as they did what he said and caused no trouble, they'd eventually be set free. 'Just so long as the Hacksville citizens think you're worth our price!' he had warned them.

Smoke from a cigar curled upwards from behind the big leather swivel chair on the other side of the desk. The outlaw leader was looking out of the window watching two men being ushered up the hill towards the house.

'Wes! Thank God,' gasped Pam, at sight of her fiancé.

'Just sit down and wait,' barked McPhee, pointing to two chairs in the corner. 'The boss is going to talk to you all when he's ready.'

'And your '*boss*' likes playing games of cat and mouse, doesn't he?' Pam said sarcastically.

But the man in the chair merely continued to smoke his cigar, much to Pam's chagrin.

There was a knock then the door was thrown open and Wheeler walked in with a gun in his hand. He waved it and gruffly called, 'In here, you two, and sit down.'

Wes and Cash Meldrum walked in, their hands tied behind their backs and their injuries all too clearly visible.

'Wes!' Pam said, distressed at the sight of her fiancé's closed eye and the bruises over his face. 'You monsters! Did you have to beat them up like that?'

Ned Slade closed the door with his heel and roughly pushed Cash down into a seat. 'It wasn't us, pretty miss,' he said, flicking his tongue suggestively over his lips. He pointed to the other chair. 'Take the weight off your feet, Diamond.' Then again to Pam, 'Guess you wouldn't know which one won, huh?'

'Pam, Evie, you all right?' Wes asked. Then spying the smoke curling up from the chair his tone hardened. 'Hawkeye, if you harm a hair on these ladies' heads, I'll—'

'You'll do what?' came the reply, and the chair swivelled round.

All four of the captives stared in amazement at the face that grinned at them, a cigar clenched between strong white teeth.

'Henry Logan!' exclaimed Wes.

Evelyn Bolton had started to her feet, her face suddenly drained of colour. Then she immediately swooned and fell to the floor.

Phin Bradley puffed contemplatively on his pipe as Hiram directed him as how best to load the two burros.

'Dammit, Hiram, d'you reckon we're going to fight an army campaign with all this stuff? Two old men, one of them with a shot-up leg and the other carrying twice as much weight as he should! Why the hell are we going on burros rather than horses?'

The old army quartermaster snorted contemptuously. 'We're riding burros 'cos they're strong as hell – and will take your weight!' he replied, with a good-natured dig. 'Besides, they can climb just about anyplace.'

Phin blew out a cloud of smoke. 'I hope the posse is already on their way back with the girls,' he said sadly. 'I don't think I'd wanta live if anything happened to my Pam.'

Hiram put a hand on his friend's arm. 'She'll be back, Phin, and so will Evelyn Bolton.' He shook his head. 'Because if they don't come back then I don't reckon much to the justice of the land.'

Phin stared at the bowl of his pipe. 'There doesn't seem to be much justice left in the country at the moment, Hiram. Certainly there's no law. Things are surely as bad as they can get when even a judge goes on the run.'

Hiram adjusted his spectacles. 'Come on now, Phin, we both know that Wes Talbot is out there doing what he can to get the girls. And maybe two old men might have a part to play in whatever's going on.'

Phin nodded. 'Guess you're right. At least we can feel like we're doing something to help out.'

*

When Evelyn Bolton finally came round from her faint, and was given a glass of water by McPhee, Wes Talbot voiced the thought that they had all been thinking.

'So Cash Meldrum didn't kill you?'

Henry Logan tossed his head back and laughed, the cigar still clamped between his teeth. 'Clearly not.' And then turning to the Deacon: 'Did you know the whole territory thinks you murdered me, Cash?'

The Deacon had not said a word until now. 'Actually, Henry, I did. Did me a little investigating in the saloon in Hacksville. A bar-bum was only too willing to let me wet his whistle in exchange for information. I hear tell you even closed the poor devil's eyes – whoever the poor guy that you murdered was – with silver dollars.'

Pam recoiled in shock and revulsion at the thought. She could not believe that Henry Logan, the town sheriff, a man that had often shared a meal with her and her father, had fabricated his own death, killing someone in the process. How long, she wondered, had this monster been playing a part?

Logan tapped ash off his cigar and nodded approvingly. 'It was a fine touch, don't you think, Cash?'

The Deacon shrugged. 'Clever, I admit. All

designed to point the finger of guilt at me. Just like the other killings, I guess.'

Logan smiled. 'Not all of them, Cash. You yourself managed to polish off two of our boys all on your own. I was impressed by that underwater trick and the stone throwing.'

The Deacon said nothing, so Wes asked, 'So this gang – the Rough Riders – you've been the mastermind all along? Even while—?'

'Even while I was Sheriff of Hacksville. That's right, Judge. Being the local lawman gave me the perfect opportunity to case out all the jobs that I planned for my men here.'

Ned Slade grinned. 'A real genius, ain't he?'

'And, of course, since I was the law, no one ever bothered Hacksville – until now, when it was necessary for me to leave.'

'Because I was coming for that woman?' the Deacon asked, his steely eyes fixing on Evelyn Bolton, who visibly cowered in her chair. 'I guess that you reckoned I'd recognize you, Henry.'

Logan puffed life into his cigar. Once he had it going to his satisfaction he said, 'Right again, Cash. Or right to some extent. You see, I needed to get you here – and that meant kidnapping Mrs Bolton. She was the perfect bait!' He beamed as he relished recounting his dastardly plan. 'Both she and the judge here. I figure that you feel you owe them something.'

Cash Meldrum's eyes flashed between Wes and

Evie, but he said nothing.

Wes shuffled in his chair. 'So now that you've admitted to being a liar, a thief and a murderer, why don't you explain just why you were so keen to entice the Deacon, a bounty hunter into your camp?'

Logan blew a slow stream of smoke from his lips. 'Oh, Cash and I go back a long way,' he explained. 'We both rode for a gang in Texas. Our last job, our richest ever, was an army payroll on its way to Fort Worth. Only thing is that the army boys didn't take too kindly to it and ran down the whole gang – except for Cash and me. All of the boys either got shot or hanged.'

The Deacon sneered. 'And I got a bullet in the back from a treacherous dog who favoured a Le Mat.'

The former Sheriff of Hacksville slowly drew his sidearm, a duplicate of the Le Mat revolver that he had left on the charred body in the Hacksville jail. 'Only you were always fast with a gun, Cash. You creased my head and knocked me cold. Then you left with the gold.'

'I oughta have made sure I'd killed you when I had the chance,' the Deacon continued. 'As it was I was losing blood and had to get away fast before the army caught up with me.'

Logan's eyes gleamed feverishly. 'But the gold, Cash. Where's the gold?'

The Deacon shook his head. 'The pursuit of

gold is the pursuit of fools. I ain't planning to make you any more foolish than you already are.'

Logan sat back and nodded his head. 'I figured you'd say something like that. Just like I figure that a little friendly torture wouldn't help any.' He sat forward, a malicious smile creeping over his face. 'But revenge, Cash? What about revenge?' He stubbed out his cigar and brushed a few flakes of ash from the desk in front of him. 'Here's the deal: you take us to the gold now, and you can have – them!'

The Deacon said nothing for a moment, then he looked at Wes, then at Evelyn Bolton, his eyes seeming to burn into her soul, like hot coals.

'It's a deal!'

TEN

After a hasty breakfast of McPhee's porridge laced with whiskey and washed down with a couple of mugs of strong black coffee, Wes felt himself start to come alive again. Both he and the Deacon had their hands untied for the duration of the meal, although they were kept apart from the two women, much to Evelyn's relief, such was her fear of Cash Meldrum. All the while, Slade and McPhee kept them under supervision, in different ends of the room, while Logan and Wheeler busied themselves loading up the string of horses.

'Where are your comrades in crime?' Wes asked.

Slade grinned. 'Well, Judge – don't mind if I drop the 'Diamond' now, do you? – they're kinda otherwise occupied. You heard the explosions earlier?'

'And the distant gunfire,' Wes replied.

The outlaw cocked his ear and nodded, for every now and then it was possible to hear the

131

sounds of gunfire. 'Yeah, it echoes a long way through the canyons, doesn't it. It's a good sign for us, 'cos as long as it goes on, we know we've got plenty of time. At least that's what the boss reckons, and he's never wrong.'

Wes nodded comprehendingly. 'So you've got the gang fighting it out with a posse or the army, while you are all preparing to go with the gang's assets.'

Ned Slade laughed. 'I knew you were a smart man, Judge. As smart as Diamond Jack, at any rate. Yeah, we'll be long gone with all the loot before they get back and realize they've been . . . taken for a ride!'

'Honour among thieves, as they say,' said the Deacon.

McPhee took a hefty swig from a hip flask. 'You could say that, laddie,' he said, wiping his lips on his sleeve. 'On the other hand, since you'll be sort of helping us to your gold, you'll be doing the honourable thing and handing it over.'

Both he and Slade guffawed at the joke.

Wes forced one of his Diamond Jack grins. 'But do you really believe that this thief,' he said, pointing to the Deacon, 'will be any more honourable than the rest of you?'

Cash Meldrum sat upright and stared at Wes with icy-cold eyes. 'I ain't no thief – not now anyways. I follow the path of the Lord.'

Wes sneered, 'By killing for a living!'

'Only those that the law – *your* law, Judge – has decreed unfit to live.'

Logan and Wheeler came in with about a half-dozen sticks of dynamite, detonators and fuse wires. 'Watch out, Wes,' Logan said cheerfully, as he began setting booby-trap wires to detonators. 'You're a judge on the run. A wanted man – dead or alive by now, I guess. Fair game for the Deacon.'

The bounty hunter grinned at this. 'That's right, just as soon as I fill my part of the bargain, you're mine, Judge!'

Wheeler clicked his tongue doubtfully. 'How do you know that you can trust this bounty hunter, boss? How come he's going to just hand over this fortune in gold?'

Logan struck flame to a cigar and puffed leisurely. 'Because we've got something that Cash holds above fortune – the means of his revenge!'

'Yeah, *Vengeance is mine; I will repay, saith the Lord* – Epistle to the Romans, Chapter 12, Verse 19.'

Evelyn Bolton sobbed and threw her arms about Pam's neck. Pam hugged her friend. 'Don't worry, Evie, I won't let him get you.'

The Deacon smiled with disdain.

The sun was rising high and turning the canyon into a roasting box with neither shelter nor shadow. The horses had been unable to keep going and had all been picked off, as were their riders, except for Red O'Leary. He, too, was now ensconced behind his dead mount. Of the four wounded men, two had slowly bled to death. Dexter Bolton had somehow managed to staunch his blood loss with a makeshift tourniquet made out of his horse's bridle.

'How's everyone holding out?' Ben Taverner called out. 'We're gonna have to make our water last until nightfall.'

And then what? Dexter Bolton wondered. Are we gonna fly outa here like bats?

'Boss, you reckon we oughta surrender?' Red O'Leary queried. 'Maybe try a white flag?'

'With these vermin?' Ben Taverner returned angrily. 'They're here to wipe us out. No, we gotta ride the storm, until the military get here.'

A hail of bullets dug up earth and ricocheted off rocks around the rancher, then a voice called out from the rim rock, 'You boys running out of water and ammo? Wanna surrender and go on home? Just put up your hands, throw down your weapons and we'll help you up.'

Dan Block, who had been hit in the thigh and was near delirious in the rising heat, threw out his weapon and struggled to his feet. 'Don't – don't shoot,' he called, as he hobbled into the open with his hands raised above his head.

A fusillade of fire from at least six directions cut him down and he died before his body hit the ground.

Mocking laughter echoed round the canyon.

'You murdering bastards!' yelled Ben Taverner.

'Hope the rest of you have said your prayers,' came the taunting voice of Hawkeye. 'Me and the boys are betting on which one of you will last longest. We've got something special in mind for him!'

Dexter Bolton was at that moment deep in prayer.

The small group rode out of Rough Valley in strict order. First the two women under the watchful eye of McPhee, then Wes and Cash Meldrum, flanked by Slade and Wheeler, then Logan and the string of horses laden with the Rough Riders' booty. Logan's hand never strayed far from the heavy Le Mat at his side.

Wes guessed that not even the outlaw gang would know where they had gone, so convoluted was the trail that Logan had chosen. They had started by riding a rivulet upstream until it reached a pool, then actually passing through the curtain of a waterfall that cascaded over the entrance to a cave. It was in fact a tunnel which some primeval river had once cut through the rock, presumably before some sort of natural silting up had diverted its course. Finding it would be a matter of pure luck, as indeed it had been when Henry Logan first discovered it some years before.

By afternoon they had reached the southern side of the Pintos and passed through a couple of miles of juniper and spruce forest, then Cash Meldrum began to direct them. He took them over land which presented a multiplicity of character. Miniature deserts gave way to brush-filled draws, then over a red rock-covered range towards the border.

As evening shadows fell, bringing a merciful drop in temperature after the scorching heat of the passage, they made camp and dined on roast jack-rabbit cooked over a fire of mesquite coals. McPhee's culinary skills at any other time would have been welcome, but for the captives, tied as they were at the wrists it was mere fuel to keep them going.

'Why did you choose this god-forsaken land, Cash?' Logan asked, as he drank coffee laced with McPhee's whiskey.

'Because it *was* god-forsaken,' the Deacon replied. 'But God is everywhere, which is what you'll find out when your time comes.'

Wes shook his head. 'Strange words for someone with murder in his heart.'

The bounty hunter looked up sharply and snapped back, 'You murdered my brother – Judge!'

'You're a blind man,' returned Wes. 'Your brother was a proven rapist and a murderer.'

Meldrum shot to his feet, his wrists straining at the rope. 'That's a damned lie! Just ask that lying bitch!'

Evelyn Bolton stared at him in speechless terror, then burst into a fit of hysterics that sent the outlaws into peals of cruel laughter.

'I thought you were going to ask her yourself, Cash – after you lead us to the gold,' said Logan, with an evil leer at Evelyn.

Parched throats, exposed skin lifting into blisters from the scorching heat, the onset of sundown offered slight relief to the survivors of the box canyon massacre. They could hear semi-drunken laughter from above, permeated every now and then by sporadic gunshots aimed at no one in particular, just let off to scare and hound.

'D'you reckon we're gonna get out of here, boss?' Roddie Pool asked.

Ever the optimist, something in his bullish personality would not even countenance the idea of defeat, Ben Taverner grunted assent. ' 'Course we will, Roddie. Morning will show a different picture.'

'You're wrong Taverner,' Dexter said angrily. 'Just like you've been wrong about everything so far. We're all going to die here. And I'm never going to see my Evie again.'

Red O'Leary shared some of his boss's optimism. 'The boss is right, Dexter. We're going to get out of here, and when we do you'll see your woman.'

'Good man,' Ben Taverner said. 'I ain't ready to

die, I've got a damned fine fiancée waiting at home for me.'

Red laughed softly. 'And I'm going to ask Laura Green to marry me. Maybe we oughta have a joint wedding, boss?'

Roddie smirked. 'Guess that makes me the only single feller here. Guess I'm going to have a good time when I get back without any competition.'

'That's the spirit, Roddie,' laughed Ben Taverner.

Dexter snorted with disdain. 'You're all mad! Mad as skunks.'

And for some reason that seemed to provoke laughter in the other three, laughter that Dexter himself found inexplicably infectious. Within moments they were all three guffawing merrily, as if their plight had been temporarily forgotten.

Then the unexpected happened. From somewhere up above a bugle sounded, ringing out the familiar sound of a cavalry charge. Rapid gunfire rang out followed by many a scream and yell as rapid-fire bullets struck home, dishing out death to many of the outlaw band.

An explosion flared on the rim rock and earth, rock and bodies went soaring over the top.

'The army! My God, I've never been so glad to hear them coming in all my life,' cried Ben Taverner.

The staccato noise of rapid, almost mechanically precise gunfire continued for a few more moments, then suddenly stopped. Then a bugle call came for ceasefire.

'You men OK down there?' called out a familiar voice.

'Phin Bradley!' gasped Dexter. He put his hands to his mouth and yelled back. 'Is that you, Phin?'

Two figures appeared outlined against the sky atop the rim rock.

'That's me, Dexter,' called out the town newspaperman. 'Me and Hiram G. Lanchester. Dynamite throwers extraordinary!'

Hiram G, the old army quartermaster turned storekeeper, had an army cap on his head and a bugle hung round his neck. 'Hacksville's very own two-man cavalry unit,' he called down. 'I always felt guilty about keeping that Gatling gun when I left the army, but I kinda hoped it'd come in useful one day.'

'And it sure did!' shouted Phin. 'Now you all know what the G in Hiram's name stands for!'

Ben Taverner stood up and laughed. 'What'd I tell you, boys? I knew we'd find a way out of this mess.'

'Well, your fortune's down there in San Miguel,' said Cash Meldrum, pointing down from the mesa to the small village surrounded by arable strip farms and pens containing milk cattle. Whitewashed adobe houses surrounded a central church with a square bell tower topped with a large wooden cross.

'So you buried it in a village, not out in the middle of the desert, eh Cash?' Logan asked.

'Ever hear the expression about hiding a tree in a forest? Well, I buried gold in a mountain of gold.'

Wheeler spat tobacco juice on the ground. 'Don't call this a mountain of no kind of gold.'

'The people down there are gold,' the Deacon replied. 'The whole fortune is in the heart of that village.'

'So this place is close to your heart, right,' said Logan. 'I'm guessing that soft spot you always had for those born south of the border finally did for you. A woman, huh?'

The Deacon shook his head. 'No woman, just the people.'

Slade grinned maliciously. 'So I guess you wouldn't want anyone down there to get hurt?'

Cash Meldrum turned gimlet eyes on the young outlaw. 'Not on my account.'

Logan lit another cigar. 'Then lead on, Cash.'

But Meldrum shook his head and raised his hands. 'Not like this. These people know me. If you want your fortune you're going to have to let us all ride down there like we was free and all friends.'

Logan chewed his cigar, then nodded to Slade. 'Cut them loose. But all of you listen up: Cash and the judge go first, followed by me and Slade. Then the two women, followed by Wheeler and McPhee.

140

If either of the men try anything, Slade and I will shoot them down and Mcphee and Wheeler will deal with the women.' He puffed contentedly on his cigar, like a man well satisfied with arrangements. 'So we've all got something to gain here from being proper friendly.'

Not long into their descent from the mesa, the church bell began to peal out, and villagers – men, women and children – appeared from their farms, houses and shops to look up at the approaching party. By the time they had reached the bottom of the zigzag trail down from the mesa a considerable welcome party had assembled, many of the men carrying pitchforks, machetes and scythes. One or two seemed to be shouldering archaic-looking rifles.

Wes's swollen eye had gone down overnight and he could now just about see out of it. He eyed Logan distastefully. 'Just consider this, Henry,' he said warningly, 'you're riding into a god-fearing community. Maybe you ought to consider giving yourself up to justice.'

Logan guffawed. 'Darn it, Judge, don't tell me that you're getting religion too!' Then, to the Deacon, 'Just how come you turned all religious anyway, Cash?'

Up ahead, some of the children had started to cheer as the party came close enough for them to recognize the Deacon.

'There's your answer,' Cash Meldrum said.

'These folks are the salt of the earth. After I stopped your bullet I somehow made it across the border, although I was damned near dead by the time I got here. Blood-poison on top of lead-poison, I guess. There was virtually nothing here. A few dirt farmers, a stack of starving kids and a sad old padre ministering to their spiritual needs from a ramshackle old mission. He took me in, dug out the bullet and treated the infection. The farm women fed me up.'

There was silence for a moment, then Logan blew smoke and shrugged. 'That it? That gave you religion?'

They were on the outskirts of the village now. Cash Meldrum pointed to a man who had come out of the church door. He was bald, in his mid-fifties, well fed with a goatee beard and dressed in a white cassock tied round the middle with a red cord. 'That's the man who converted me. He showed me the way that God works through good people.'

'Señor Cash, you have returned,' cried the priest, picking up the hem of his cassock and hurrying to meet the party. 'And you have brought friends, yes?'

Meldrum dismounted and embraced the padre, the crowd of villagers swamping them, eager it seemed to touch and greet the Deacon, like some respected senior member of their community who had not been seen for a long time.

'Father Rodriguez, I have brought a band of pilgrims to see the treasure of San Miguel. Mind if I show them?'

The padre beamed and went from one to the other shaking hands and blessing each person in the procession. 'You will all have dinner with me this evening,' he announced. 'I see that some of you have had injuries that we can tend to. It can be a bad journey across the Pintos.' He nodded at the villagers, signalling to two or three of the village elders to follow him. 'We will make preparations while Señor Cash, my good friend and son, shows you our little church. Our village will always be grateful to him. If he is your friend, then you are blessed to know him.'

He left, ushering the village elders before him and leaving the group free to enter the church. They dismounted and approached it, the outlaws with their hands on their gun handles. At the door, Logan turned to McPhee and Wheeler. 'You two keep watch outside – just in case of any trouble – from within or without.'

ELEVEN

Logan urged the group down the aisle of the church towards the altar while Slade closed the door after them.

The Deacon bowed in front of the large golden crucifix and genuflected. Then standing and raising his arms to indicate the décor of the church, with its stained glass windows depicting the life of St Michael, the gleaming lectern, offertory candles and plates upon the altar, he smiled and said, 'Isn't it beautiful?'

Logan nodded. 'Almost like some sorta cathedral, rather than some peasant village church.'

'They aren't peasants,' Cash Meldrum corrected. 'They're honest farmers and shopkeepers. They're all doing their best and making it work.'

'Whatever you think, Cash,' said Logan impatiently. 'Now suppose you just get the gold for us.'

The Deacon smiled wanly. 'Your fortune is right

here, Henry. All around you. This church, the mission house, the school, the farm tools, crops and cattle. The Lord has provided all this bounty.'

Slade had produced his gun again. 'The only bounty I see is the one standing in front of us now, lying through his teeth.'

The Deacon eyed the outlaw through gimlet eyes. 'I never lie in God's house, kid. Remember that.' He pointed to the gun. 'And weapons ain't allowed in here.'

'The hell they ain't!' returned Slade. 'Do you want me to persuade him some, boss?'

Henry Logan pursed his lips then shook his head. 'Not yet, Slade. Not until he's explained some. What do you mean, Cash, it's all around?'

'Just what I said. I gave these people the money. Everything, every last cent. Father Rodriguez and these people took me in when I was half dead and showed me that there was a better way than stealing and cheating. They didn't ask for anything, they just gave.' His face creased into the nearest he could come to a smile. 'So I gave them the gold. This town and the people are your fortune, Henry.'

'You mean you staked them?' queried Logan, incredulously. 'You gave them a fortune to build a church and a few damned houses? You didn't get religion, Meldrum, you got madness.'

Slade pointed to one of the candlesticks. 'So how're we gonna get it all back? We gonna load it

145

up on the horses, or should we take one of these dirt farmer's carts?'

'You'll touch nothing!' the Deacon stated.

'I think we'll decide on that,' Logan corrected.

'So you're going to add church-robbing to your crimes,' Wes said, contemptuously. 'Have you no shame?'

The Deacon smirked. 'You're a fine one to talk about shame, Judge. You had an innocent man hanged. Still, you're mine now.' He turned to Logan and held out a hand. 'I've completed my part, Henry. I've shown you the fortune. Now give me a gun.'

Logan tossed back his head and laughed. 'Cash, you expect me to just be satisfied with *seeing* how you squandered my gold? That beats all, sure enough. No, there's no way you're having a gun until we're long out of here with as much money as we can muster.'

'And how are we gonna get this fortune, boss?' Slade asked impatiently. 'You heard him, they used the money to build this town. Are we gonna carry off walls, coloured glass and everything? Seems to me the only useful things are these gold and silver church ornaments that can be melted down.'

'Like I said,' went on the Deacon, 'you ain't taking anything. And I want a gun to deal with this judge and that lying bitch.'

Logan smiled. 'Now what was that you said about no weapons in church, Cash? Forget it, and just cut all this crap and show me the real money.'

The Deacon advanced towards Evelyn Bolton. 'Then I'll take her outside now.'

Sure that Evelyn would be terrified, Pam stepped between the Deacon and her friend. She was shocked to feel Evelyn put a hand on her shoulder and push her aside.

'I've had enough of this bully-boy bounty hunter,' Evelyn said, standing her ground, arms akimbo. 'He's wasted enough of our time, Henry. Shoot him now and be done with it!'

Wes, Pam and Cash Meldrum stood stock-still and stared in astonishment.

'Evie?' Pam gasped. 'What – what are you saying?'

Logan and Slade were laughing cruelly, as if a long-standing joke had finally been discovered, and the perpetrator was exasperated by the gulli- bility of the people she had been hoodwinking.

'What do you think it means, Miss Goody Two- shoes?' Evelyn Bolton replied sarcastically. 'It means that Henry and I are – older friends than you fools thought.'

The former Hacksville sheriff grinned. 'Not exactly man and wife, but as near as can be. We've shared more than just a bed for a lot of years.'

Wes nodded. 'You mean that she's been feeding you with information about Dexter Bolton's bank clients?'

Logan smiled. 'A superb team, we've been.

Evelyn was able to tell me things about folks that even I didn't know as the town sheriff. I was able to plan the heists at leisure.'

'And me and the boys carried them out,' added Slade with a chuckle.

'So you're admitting that my brother never touched you?' Cash Meldrum demanded. 'There never was any robbery? No rape?'

Henry Logan answered on her behalf. 'Well, there was a robbery, which the boys carried out, but no rape. It was all part of the plan, Cash. I heard tell that your brother got hisself a job riding guard. The rape story enabled us to get the judge here involved. Naturally you wouldn't believe your brother was a killer or a rapist, so you'd be bound to come looking for revenge. News of a hanging gets around fast, so it was about the best way we could get you to come outa the woodwork.'

The Deacon looked incredulously at Wes, then back at Logan. 'My little brother was killed so as you could induce me to come looking for revenge?'

Henry grinned, obviously proud of the way his devious masterplan had worked out. 'That's right. And Evelyn here was the bait. Of course, we had to get her out of Hacksville, so Slade here kidnapped her.'

'Then I was just taken too by mistake?' Pam asked, almost unable to believe that Evelyn Bolton was not the friend she had always thought her to be.

Logan shook his head. 'Not at all! It was all planned to perfection. We took you to make sure that the judge here followed on. He was the other part of the bait; I knew that Cash would be so riddled with hatred for him.'

Wes was badly shaken by these revelations. 'So you knew all along that Daniel Meldrum was an innocent man?' He looked at Evelyn Bolton with utter disgust. 'And you lied in order to get an innocent man hanged? What kind of woman are you?'

Evelyn Bolton tossed back her head and laughed, then stared him straight in the eye and replied defiantly, 'I'm Logan's woman! I'm like him and I'll do anything to get what I want. I even slept with that worm Dexter for two years,' she said, with a squirm of revulsion at the mere mention of her legal husband.

'You're a monster!' said Pam.

Evelyn Bolton shrugged dismissively. 'Logan, I've had enough of this. Let's cut our losses and get out of here. Tell Slade to shoot them all.'

Slade grunted and pulled back the hammer of his gun. 'I don't take orders from a woman,' he said, 'but I kinda agree, it's time we got moving.'

The shot rang out deafeningly in the church. An expression of astonishment registered on Ned Slade's face and he looked down to see an expanding patch of blood on his shirt-front.

'Sorry, Slade,' said Henry Logan, the barrel of his Le Mat smoking. 'You're one too many.'

Slade winced as the pain and realization of his death suddenly dawned on him. Then with a bizarre smile, as if at the moment of his death he saw something humorous in this whole thing, his eyes rolled and he fell forward, his gun falling from his lifeless fingers.

'Kill them all, Logan!' cried the outlaw's woman.

Pam stared in horror at her former friend, all her pent-up fury suddenly erupting in volcanic flow. 'You she-devil! You did all this!' And with a swipe, she punched her in the mouth, immediately following up with a kick on the shin. Then she jumped on her, grabbing her hair as they fell to the floor in a mass of kicking legs and flailing fists.

Logan had watched and hesitated just long enough to allow Cash Meldrum to reach the altar and grab the offertory plate, which he sent hurling discus-fashion at Logan. The former sheriff ducked, but not quite fast enough and the plate caught him a glancing blow on the side of the temple and he keeled over into the aisle.

Meldrum picked up Slade's gun and fired a shot at the two women as they rolled about on the floor. It hit the ground between them, gouging out splinters that showered their faces.

'Get up!' Meldrum barked. And before Wes could make a move, the Deacon swung the gun at him and ratcheted the hammer back. 'Don't even think about it, Judge.'

From outside there came the noise of a crowd

shouting and of shots being fired.

The Deacon swung the gun back towards Evelyn Bolton, who stared at him with horror-stricken eyes. 'Don't – don't shoot! Logan made me do it. I'll do anything you want. I'll do anything for you. I'll be your—'

Cash Meldrum eyed her distastefully, as the noise outside increased and more shots rang out. 'You are truly the most disgusting woman I ever met. You sent my brother to his death and you knew he wasn't guilty of anything.'

Wes took a step nearer. 'Don't do anything stupid, Meldrum,' he said. 'Put the gun down. We've heard their confessions, both hers and Logan's. Let the law deal with them. You'll get justice for your brother: the chances are they'll both hang.'

The Deacon sneered. 'The law! It ain't going to bring back my brother, is it?' He flicked his tongue over dry lips. 'An eye for an eye!'

Evelyn backed into the wall, her hands outstretched, tears running down her beautiful cheeks. 'Please, I'll do anything.'

'Prepare to see Hell!' said the Deacon.

Another shot rang out and the Deacon shook as if he had been dealt a sudden blow in the sternum. Henry Logan climbed to his feet, his Le Mat smoking again. 'Damn you, Cash! It didn't have to be like this.' And he fired two more bullets into the Deacon's chest.

Each time Cash Meldrum reeled backwards and he tottered on his feet, but he did not go down. Instead, he slowly raised the gun at Evelyn Bolton.

'Dammit Logan! Shoot him!' Evelyn screamed.

Blood trickled from the corner of Cash's mouth, which twisted into a smile. 'Come see Satan with me!' And he fired, shooting her through the heart.

'L-Logan!' she mouthed, her eyes wide as she slumped back, before sliding lifelessly to the floor, dragging a blood trail down the adobe wall after her.

'No!' bellowed Logan, firing three more shots into Cash's chest, then, changing tactic as his body refused to drop, he shot him in the head. The bounty hunter fell backwards, stone dead.

Pam stared aghast at Evelyn Bolton's body. Logan had taken a couple of faltering steps towards her, his face ashen. Then he looked at Pam, as if her presence suddenly reminded him that he was not yet done. Wes divined his thought and dived for the gun that had fallen from the Deacon's grip.

Logan's gun barked again, a bullet sending Deacon's gun sliding across the floor before Wes could clasp it. Wes pushed himself painfully into a crouch. 'Listen, Logan, come with us. You could plead madness. I can't promise anything, but—'

'I've lost Evelyn!' Logan snapped back. Then a sick grin came to his lips. 'But I've still got more money than I'll ever need.' He adjusted the hammer of the Le Mat, so that it brought the shotgun barrel into operation. 'I'm truly sorry about this, Wes,' he said, raising the Le Mat and pointing straight at Wes's chest. 'I really did like you.'

Wes jolted as the noise of the gunshot rang out. But on looking down at his chest, to his amazement he saw no blood, no wound, felt no pain.

Blood streamed from a hole in Henry Logan's forehead and he fell forward, the big Le Mat discharging as he fell. A pew exploded into splinters beside Wes.

Pam was standing with Slade's smoking gun held in both hands.

The church doors burst open and Father Rodriguez and a group of villagers rushed in, bloody knives and sickles in their hands telling of the short work they had made of Wheeler and McPhee.

'*Madre mia*!' gasped the padre, genuflecting as he came quickly up the aisle to see the supine body of the Deacon.

'Wes, I – I—' Pam began, her whole body trembling. The judge enveloped her in his arms. 'It's over, Pam,' he whispered in her ear. 'It's over.'

That evening Father Rodriguez was as good as his word and Wes and Pam dined with him. It was a sombre, cheerless meal after all that had happened. The old priest had listened to their explanation of the carnage that had unfolded in the little church and translated for the villagers, who had deferentially removed the body of Cash Meldrum and Evelyn Bolton, and somewhat less respectfully the bodies of Henry Logan and the other outlaws. And as was the custom in the village, which had no law as such, the bodies were buried swiftly in the small cemetery behind the church. Despite their obvious grief for Cash Meldrum, they conducted themselves with decorum.

As they sat round Father Rodriguez's simple square table, Pam mused, 'I can't believe that Evelyn was—'

'Not the friend you thought?' Wes finished for her. He shook his head. 'The same goes for Henry Logan. I'd always thought of him as a square man and it was a shock to find that he wasn't dead after all.'

Father Rodriguez poured more wine as they finished their food. 'I am sad for you both, my friends,' he said. 'San Miguel has much to thank Señor Cash for, but somehow we always expected that something bad would happen to him.' He sipped his wine, pensively. 'He told us that one day he may come with men and that he would tell us that he was bringing pilgrims to see the treasure of San Miguel. That would be the sign that he was in trouble and that we would have to act.'

Pam stopped with her wineglass halfway to her

lips. 'So he had a plan?'

The padre nodded, with a sigh. 'But we were still too slow. We could not save him.' He crossed his chest. 'There has been too much blood spilled today.'

'That is true, Father Rodriguez,' Wes said. 'But if it is any consolation, I believe that Cash Meldrum would feel that he got justice for his brother.'

The padre smiled drily. 'No my friend, he *avenged* his brother: the Lord will consider whether justice was done or not.'

They left the following morning with two of the villagers, to give them safe passage across the border and through the Pintos. It was an arduous journey, but one that was eased when they ran into a platoon of the US Cavalry, which was scouring the Pintos for the remains of the Rough Riders' outfit. With the army protection they bade farewell to the San Miguel villagers and travelled back to Hacksville with the outlaw spoils, where Wes arranged for the stolen hoard to be lodged in the Hacksville bank until it could be officially and legally transferred back to the rightful owners. Then Wes set in force the official documentation giving Daniel Meldrum a posthumous pardon. The full story was duly published as an exclusive by Phin Bradley in the *Hacksville Chronicle* and circulated throughout the territory.

The multiple funerals for the Hacksville posse

members was a sad and traumatic occasion for the whole town. All of the congregation were subdued, especially Dexter Bolton, who was crushed by the revelations about Evelyn and Henry Logan.

'I'm going back East,' he announced after the funeral.

'The hell you are, Dexter,' said Phin. 'We need you right here, running the best bank in the Southwest.'

'That's right,' agreed Hiram G. 'We've got a town to build again and we need you to help us build back its dignity.'

Ben Taverner also threw his weight into trying to persuade the banker. Like Dexter he had received a blow to his ego when he returned to find that Betsy and her friend Laura had already left town for safer and less dangerous pastures. No longer was he puffed up with his own importance, for he had learned humility.

'You've got to stay, Dexter,' he said. 'We've got the makings of a great little town here. We've got honest people at the helm now: you looking after our money and Red O'Leary looking after the law.'

Phin had looked at Wes. 'And the answer to that question you were about to ask me, is yes. You'll make my Pam a good husband, I know.'

Wes thanked the newspaperman, but before he and Pam started making plans for their wedding he still had work to do.

*

A week later Wes and Pam stood in the little ceme-tery at San Miguel, watching as Father Rodriguez conducted yet another funeral. Wes had arranged for the exhumation of the body of Daniel Meldrum from the executed felons' cemetery at the state penitentiary and its transportation to San Miguel, where his body was reinterred beside that of his brother, Cash.

'The law failed you both,' Wes said, as he stood at the twin graves after the ceremony. 'I feel bad about the way this all turned out, and that's some-thing I'm going to have to carry with me until the day that I die.' He laid flowers on each grave. 'Bringing you together is the best I can do to make amends. Cash tried to look out for you, Daniel, after your death, now maybe he can look out for you in the hereafter.'

And as Pam and he walked away, Pam placed flowers on her former friend's grave. 'I know she was bad, Wes, but somehow I can't believe that there wasn't at least some spark of good in her. I'll never forget the way she died.' Then taking his hand she asked, 'Is it really over now, Wes? Can we get away from this saga of stealing and killing?'

He took her in his arms and nodded. 'It's over, Pam. I'm relieved to be back on the right side of the law again. Now we can think about us.'

'I'm never going to let you go on the run again. From now on you're a watched man.'

He laughed, and then kissed her lovingly. 'That sounds like you're passing sentence on me, Pam.'

She hugged him. 'That's right, Judge Talbot. I'm giving you a life sentence – with me!'